SHERLOCK BONES

AND THE CASE OF THE CROWN JEWELS

Published in Great Britain in 2022 by Buster Books,
an imprint of Michael O'Mara Books Limited,
9 Lion Yard, Tremadoc Road, London SW4 7NQ

W www.mombooks.com/buster

f Buster Books

🐦 @BusterBooks

📷 buster_books

A CIP catalogue record for this book is available from the British Library.

ISBN: 978-1-78055-750-2

1 3 5 7 9 10 8 6 4 2

Papers used by Buster Books are natural, recyclable products
made of wood from well-managed, FSC®-certified forests and
other controlled sources. The manufacturing processes conform
to the environmental regulations of the country of origin.

This book was printed in April 2022 by
CPI Group (UK) Ltd, 108 Beddington Lane,
Croydon, CR0 4YY, United Kingdom.

MIX
Paper from
responsible sources
FSC
www.fsc.org
FSC® C171272

SHERLOCK BONES
AND THE CASE OF THE CROWN JEWELS

Written by Tim Collins
Illustrated by John Bigwood

Buster Books

With additional artwork by
Stracioni and Alan Brown

Edited by Frances Evans
Designed by Derrian Bradder
Cover design by John Bigwood

Welcome

Sherlock Bones and Dr Jane Catson are world-famous for solving crimes. Each case is written down by Catson, so you can read all about their adventures.

Sherlock Bones

Sherlock Bones is the greatest detective the world has ever known. He never runs away from a puzzle, and always cracks his cases.

Dr Jane Catson

Dr Jane Catson is Sherlock Bones' crime-fighting partner. She's always ready to pounce into action when faced with a sneaky criminal.

Are you ready to help Bones and Catson solve their trickiest case yet? Throughout the story, you will find puzzles where you can put your detective skills to the test. If you get stuck, you can find all the answers at the back of the book, starting on page 169. You can also just enjoy reading the adventure and come back to the puzzles later if you want to. Good luck!

Chapter One

"I need a case that will challenge me," said Sherlock Bones. "Something I can really puzzle over."

My friend was slouching back in his chair with his head propped on his paws, surrounded by chewed rubber toys and old packets of dog biscuits. Bones is unstoppable when he's solving a crime. He darts around with his black nose twitching, restlessly searching for clues. But when his skills aren't needed, he sits around for days on end, gloomy and hardly moving at all.

"I'm sure something will come along," I said.

I was trying to sound positive, but I had to admit that things had been very quiet recently. Everyone knows that if you have a tricky problem, you come to Sherlock Bones and Dr Catson's detective agency. But we'd had no visitors for almost a week.

I glanced through my newspaper, *The Morning Terrier*, to see if any crimes had been reported. The first few pages were taken up with pictures of royal dogs and celebrity foxes, but I found something promising further in.

Can you work out which story has caught Catson's attention? The letters in the word finder puzzle below can be rearranged to spell a word that will give you a clue.

PUZZLE CORNER
TEATIME TEASERS

ROYAL REPORT
With our royal correspondent, Ashley Sloper

WORD FINDER

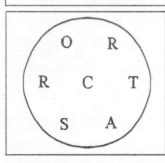

O
R
R
C
T
S
A

The royal slippers, which have been in the family since the days of King Charles the Spaniel, had been placed at the end of Her Majesty's bed by her loyal butler, Jenkins. Prince Rex made off with the left one yesterday afternoon and set about chomping on it.

Word from the palace is that one particular pup has been a bad, bad boy. That's right, young Prince Rex, the grandson of the Queen, was caught gnawing on a very precious item of footwear.

The slipper in question is said to be beyond repair, and our sources tell us that the young prince was sent to his basket with no dinner.

PRICELESS HEIRLOOM STOLEN

A dog from Kennel Heights has had a family heirloom stolen. Butch Rover, a carpenter who specializes in houses for large dogs, claims his pocket watch was taken on Wednesday night.

"It's been in my family for generations," said the dog. "I feel lost without it."

When asked if he'd glimpsed the thief, Butch broke down in tears and refused to speak. After his sobbing had ceased, the dog claimed the experience was so terrifying he

Butch Rover – carpenter and victim of theft

Pocket watch and family heirloom stolen

didn't want to think about it.

The usually quiet area of Kennel Heights has suffered a wave of crime in the last few

weeks. A wedding ring, two silver brooches and a gold medal have all been reported missing.

"We have the situation under control,"

commented Inspector Bloodhound. "Rest assured, we have our finest young officers working on it."

Report by Ginger Pawson

It will be a fine, clear morning, so expect disruption on bridges as otters line up to dive into the river.

The weather will turn cooler in the afternoon, and by evening, a fog will sweep in, so take extra care if you're venturing out.

Tomorrow will bring more hot weather, so it is recommended that you keep your windows open at night.

MYSTERY AT THE DOCKS

A large shipment of carrots has gone missing from the docks. They were housed in a Swedish container ship, waiting for inspection by officials.

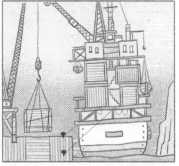

This is the latest in a long line of carrot thefts that have plagued the city in the last few weeks. Could they be related to the 'Carrot Tax', an extra charge on carrots introduced by the government last year? Not according to minister Rocky Walker.

"I doubt this has anything to do with the new tax," said Walker. "Rabbits understand that they must contribute just like everyone else. I pay tax on my squeaky toys and collars, so why shouldn't they pay it on their carrots? Now if you'll excuse me, I have a stick to fetch."

But the tax remains deeply unpopular with rabbits on the street. Our poll last week revealed that as many as 50% of them would consider buying illegal carrots to avoid it.

LOCAL MOLE HAS RECORD-BREAKING COLLECTION

It's official – Mr A. F. Gibson has the largest collection of royal souvenirs in the world. Inspectors from the World Record Association have visited his shop in Kitten Mews and confirmed that his selection of memorabilia is bigger than any they've ever seen.

"I've always suspected I had the best collection of royal gifts," said Gibson. "And to have it confirmed is just wonderful."

To celebrate the record, Mr Gibson is offering 20% off royal toilet-roll holders to anyone who brings a copy of this article to his shop today.

"I'll tell you what," he said. "Buy three dog towels at the same time, and I'll make it 25%".

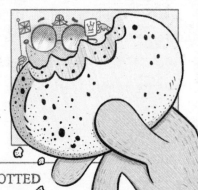

MYSTERIOUS RAT SPOTTED

"Look at this," I said, holding up the newspaper. "A shipment of Swedish carrots has gone missing from the docks. Perhaps we could look into that."

Bones glanced at the story and shrugged. "A gang of troublemaking rabbits probably took them while the guards were asleep. I'm sure the police will come to us if it turns out to be anything important."

I kept reading, desperate to find a more exciting crime. I fixed on a picture of a large, scowling Doberman.

"Look here," I said. "This dog from Kennel Heights has had his pocket watch stolen. It was a family heirloom, apparently."

Bones snatched the paper and scanned through the article. "The poor mutt probably just kicked it under his basket by mistake," he said. "I want a crime that's worthy of the front page, not page eight."

Bones threw the newspaper back to me and folded his paws. I kept looking through it, still hoping to find something that would excite him.

I looked up to see Bones leaning forward in his chair. One of his floppy black ears had pricked up.

"Do you hear that?" he asked. "Sounds like good news."

I listened. At first I could hear nothing but the usual noises, such as the chugging of cars and the stoat family from across the road yelling at each other. But then I made out the thud of approaching pawsteps, and a panting noise that gave way to a low growl.

"Someone's coming," I said. "But how do you know it's good news?"

"My dear Catson," said Bones. "It's all very simple. We can tell from the heaviness of the steps that a large dog is coming. From the panting, we know the dog is out of breath. And yet it is not running. So the dog started off at a high speed, but had to give up and walk somewhere along the way, because it had covered a long distance. And what do we make of the growls between the pants? The creature is annoyed that it has had to come here at all. Perhaps because it didn't want to visit us, but now feels it must."

The pawsteps stopped outside our kennel and I heard the animal getting its breath back.

"Of course!" I cried. "It's Inspector Bloodhound, here to ask for our help. It all seems so simple when you explain it."

I could see the outline of the large dog through our door.

Can you use this photo to work out which of the following silhouettes belongs to Inspector Bloodhound? They all look similar, but only one matches the Inspector exactly.

A.

B.

C.

The Inspector barged in. His saggy jowls were quivering and his shoulders were drooping.

"Something awful has happened," he said, still panting. "We need your help."

"Excellent," said Bones, rubbing his paws together. "Sounds like just the sort of thing I was hoping for."

The Inspector growled. "This is not a cause for celebration," he barked. "It is the most serious matter possible. In fact, it concerns the Queen!"

I gasped. We had come across some terrible criminals in our time, but never one who would dare to commit a crime against Her Majesty.

"It's the crown jewels," said the Inspector in a low voice. "The Queen placed them on her velvet cushion before going to sleep last night. When she woke up this morning, they were gone."

I'd seen the Queen wearing these jewels in a parade outside the palace a year ago. There was a golden crown studded with rubies and emeralds, a sapphire ring and a silver necklace with three dangling rows of priceless diamonds.

They were the most valuable jewels in the country. Whoever had taken them must be a dangerous villain.

Bones leapt up and paced around, clasping his paws behind his back. His tail was wagging.

"Were there any signs of a break-in at the palace?" he asked. "A forced door or smashed window, for example?"

"No," said the Inspector. "It was as if no one had been there at all."

I tried to picture our Queen when she discovered her jewels were missing. She was a pug with a droopy mouth, and looked grumpy at the best of times. She must have looked gloomier than a thundercloud when she realized the crown, ring and necklace were all gone.

"What about the guard dogs?" asked Bones. "Did they hear anything?"

"Nothing," said Inspector Bloodhound. "And they were stationed around the palace all night."

Bones came to a stop, and his tail fell still. "When did you find all this out?"

The Inspector looked down at the floor, avoiding Bones' gaze. "Seven o'clock this morning," he said.

Bones looked at the Inspector like he'd just snatched an entire string of sausages from his bowl.

"That's four hours ago!" he barked.

"I know you're going to say I should have come sooner," said the Inspector, holding his paws up. "And maybe I should have. But I wanted to give the young police pups a chance first."

"And let me guess," said Bones. "They've spent the entire time barking at each other and chasing squirrels."

"Only some of it," said the Inspector. "In fact, they've discovered no fewer than three clues. We just need a little help working out what they mean."

The Inspector puffed out his chest and patted his uniform.

"Firstly, a low rumbling noise was reported by the mole who runs the souvenir shop on Kitten Mews," he said. "Secondly, the pups discovered some strange markings on a tree in the park opposite the palace. And thirdly, they found a trail of prints leading away from a puddle on the front lawn."

Bones rushed around the room, looking for his hat and magnifying glass. "Please tell me those pups have left the prints alone instead of trampling all over them."

Can you help Bones find his hat and magnifying glass in his messy kennel?

"Well, they might have got a little overexcited," said the Inspector. "But they'd done so well to find the clues, I didn't have the heart to stop them."

"Come on, Catson!" yipped Bones, rushing out of the door. "There isn't a moment to lose."

I grabbed my hat, scarf and coat, and pelted after him. It was time for the world's greatest detective to leap into action.

Chapter Two

The grey domes of Kennel Palace loomed ahead of us as we sped through the park. It was the most magnificent building in the whole city, with five floors and over a hundred sleeping baskets. Thirty maids and butlers attended to the Queen's every wish, and fierce German shepherd guards patrolled the grounds.

As we drew closer, we could see the police bloodhound pups bounding around on the front lawn. Their baggy ears and jowls flapped as they ran in circles.

They were called Benedict, Bartholomew, Benjamin, Bibi and Bessie. The Inspector had hired them a few months before and was determined to give them experience of real investigations, even though they were far too young for it.

All their running about had churned the grass into mud. The very area we had come to examine had been turned into a shapeless mush by the silly youngsters.

"Get them away from here!" barked Bones. "I've told you before not to let those excitable fools near crime scenes!"

"That'll do, pups!" shouted Inspector Bloodhound. "We'll take it from here."

He took a rubber ball out of his pocket and threw it into the park. The police pups raced after it with their tails wagging and their pink tongues lolling.

The Inspector and I stepped back, while Bones examined what was left of the crime scene with his magnifying glass.

"This was a muddy puddle before your pups chose to use the lawn as their playground," he said, pointing to a spot next to him. "I can make out a set of prints leading away. It's possible that the thief made them as they were fleeing the palace."

He stepped carefully across the lawn to the pavement at the south side of the palace.

"The trail continues this way," he said. "Catson and I will follow it and report back to you."

"Let me know as soon as you find another clue," said the Inspector. "I'll bring the pups to help you."

Bones paced along, with his eyes on the ground. There were other trails of prints on the pavement, and he had to look very closely to follow the right one. He almost bumped into an elderly weasel, who harrumphed loudly.

"I'm sorry," I said. "You must forgive my friend."

The prints led us down to the river.

Can you help Bones and Catson find the trail of prints that will lead them to the river?

We followed the trail along the water and on to the great iron bridge that links the north and south of the city. It was filled with porcupines on bicycles, hamsters in balls and huge families of rabbits packed into cars.

Bones pushed through the crowd with his eyes still on the ground. I could see the steep hill of Kennel Heights ahead of us. This was the most expensive neighbourhood in the whole city, where giant kennels with grand porches and large windows stood over sloping lawns.

I sidestepped a group of otters to catch up with Bones.

"Surely our criminal can't live in Kennel Heights," I said. "None of the respectable folk who live there would ever steal from the Queen."

"You'll find as much slyness inside those spotless mansions as in the city's scruffiest alleys," said Bones. "More, perhaps."

A huge crowd of badgers were crammed around a worm stall on the far side of the bridge, and Bones barged right through them, almost knocking them over. Several of them growled at us.

"My apologies," I said. "We're on important business!"

The prints took us up the steep road that circled Kennel Heights, passing a three-story kennel with a marble statue of King Charles the Spaniel outside. Despite what Bones had said, I found it difficult to believe anyone who lived here would commit such a crime.

My mood wasn't helped by the speed at which Bones was racing up the hill. A few weeks of catnapping and eating too many biscuits had taken its toll on me. I was flustered and out of breath within minutes, while my friend seemed to have limitless energy.

I was about to suggest that we took a break when I noticed he'd stopped anyway. The trail had come to an end outside a huge pink kennel that was shaped like a castle, with flags waving from the turrets.

Use these clues to work out which kennel
the trail of prints has ended at:
· The kennel has a door, not a drawbridge.
· It has more than five flags but fewer than nine flags.
· It has a rectangular flag that is facing to the right.

A.

B.

C.

D.

E.

24

Bones knocked on the neat wooden door.

There was a shuffling noise from inside, and a poodle with immaculate white fur opened it. She had long, curly fur on her head, with a silver tiara perched neatly at the top, and round pompoms around her paws. A perfect white ball of fur bobbed on the end of her wagging tail.

I tried to get my breath back so I could introduce us. Bones has a habit of rudely walking into houses when he's on a case, and she didn't look like the sort of dog who'd take that well.

But before I could say anything, she stepped aside and beckoned us in.

"Sherlock Bones and Dr Catson," she said. "Just who I was hoping to see. I take it you got my message, then?"

Chapter Three

The poodle led us into a wide room with white walls and antique wooden furniture.

There were a few faded posters on the walls for old plays such as *Rover and Juliet* and *Catbeth*. The poodle herself could be seen on some, and it turned out she was an actress named Molly Ruffington. The name didn't ring a bell with me. If she'd been famous, it must have been a long time ago.

A huge glass display case covering the far wall of the room contained dozens of tiaras, all as fancy as the one Molly was wearing. Some had opals and moonstones set into them, while others had intricate roses made from pink and white diamonds. The whole cabinet was full, except for an empty space in the top right corner.

Can you pick out the following groups from Molly's tiara cabinet?

A.

B.

C.

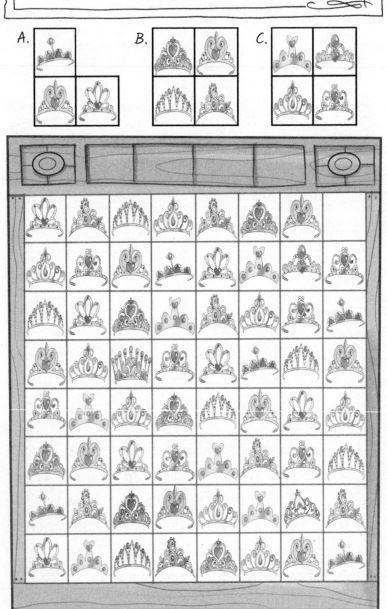

There were two long purple sofas in the room. Molly sat on one, while I perched on the end of the other, terrified of covering such expensive furniture with cat hairs.

"I'm afraid there's been some sort of mix-up," I explained. "We received no message from you."

"Oh," she said. "I gave the post stoat a note for you this morning. Perhaps he dropped it. I remembered reading about how you found the Countess of Bitechester's missing locket, and thought you might be just the detectives for my problem."

Bones fell to his paws and knees and examined Molly's feet through his magnifying glass. She shot me an uncomfortable glance.

"As a matter of fact, we're here on a very serious case indeed," Bones said, without looking up. "I'm afraid to report that the Queen's crown has been stolen."

Molly dragged the back of her paw across her forehead and howled.

"Why are there such wicked creatures in the world?" she asked. She pointed to the empty space in her display case with a trembling paw. "Something very important has been stolen from me, too. My diamond tiara, the pride of my collection, was taken from me last night!"

Molly buried her face in her paws and began to sob.

"Don't worry," said Bones. "We'll get it back for you."

"But how will you find the time to search for my burglar when you're looking for the crown thief?" she asked.

Bones stood up and put his paws behind his back.

"That might be easier than you suppose," he said. "Because I believe they could be one and the same person."

Molly gasped.

I thought back to the prints we had followed. The burglar could have taken the crown jewels from the palace and decided to continue their crime spree in Kennel Heights. What a beastly criminal they must be.

"Did you catch a glimpse of the villain?" asked Bones.

"I'm afraid not," said Molly. "I was out on my evening walk when it happened. I came home to find a trail of muddy prints leading from the door to the cabinet."

Bones dropped back to the floor and examined it through his magnifying glass.

"I cleaned them up," said Molly. "You must understand that I can't stand mess or dirt."

"I'm sure we'd all have done the same," said Bones.

I was sure we wouldn't. Our rooms in Barker Street are a mess of newspapers, string, toy birds and kitty litter. Bones considers cleaning a waste of his time and intelligence, and I refuse to do it if he doesn't.

Bones looked at the display case, chairs and walls through his magnifying glass, so it fell to me to fill the uncomfortable silence.

"Don't worry," I said. "We'll have your tiara back in no time. We've never failed to solve a case yet."

"I do hope so," said Molly. She strode over to the front door and opened it. "You've both been so kind."

I stepped outside. Bones exited on his paws and knees, still looking through his magnifying glass. He examined the garden path and kept going along the pavement.

"Thank you so much," said Molly, closing the door.

Bones took a right turn and I followed him, glancing around to see if anyone was noticing his odd behaviour. There was no one around at all, except for the post stoat, who was delivering letters from his satchel.

It was amazing how much quieter Kennel Heights was than the busy streets down in the city. It was much cleaner up there, too. You could breathe the air without feeling like you were inside a chimney, and there was no dirt on the pavements. If the trail of muddy prints had continued, we'd have been able to see them. But there was nothing.

"Looks like we've run out of clues," I said.

"Not quite," said Bones. He pointed to a scrap of paper that had fallen to the floor. It showed a picture of a scowling Doberman holding a wind-up watch. Underneath, it said:

Stolen pocket watch.
Great sentimental value.
Pat on head offered as reward.
Contact Butch at
134 Kennel Heights.

Can you put these panels in the correct order, so they form the picture of Butch the Doberman? Panel A is in the correct place to get you started.

A. B. C. D. E. F. G. H.

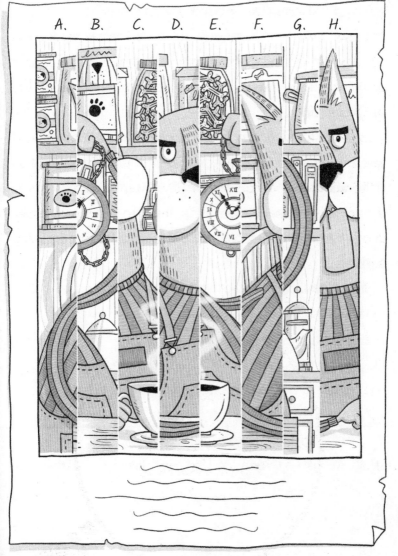

Bones got back to his feet and bounded up the road. I jogged after him. The road became even steeper, and I was glad of the rest we'd taken in Molly's house.

The road spiralled around the hill, and I looked at the wide river and sprawling roads far below us. I could see the palace and park clearly, but most of the streets were hidden behind a cloud of smog that spewed out of the factories.

Ahead of me, Bones had come to a stop. Number 134 was a wide kennel with a thick oak door. I shuddered to think about the fierce dog inside. After years of chasing dangerous criminals, there isn't much that scares me. But even I find my fur standing on end when a Doberman starts barking.

Bones climbed the steps and knocked on the door, while I stayed back, ready to bolt if things turned nasty.

A large dog with a big snout opened the door and fixed his black eyes on us. He was wearing blue overalls and had a red handkerchief poking out of his side pocket.

"What do you want?" he growled.

"It's about your missing pocket watch," said Bones. "I'm afraid we haven't found it. But we'd like to ask what you know about the thief."

The Doberman howled and sunk to the floor, covering his eyes with his paws.

"He's not coming back, is he?" he yelped. "Please don't let him come back!"

Chapter Four

We assured Butch that the thief wasn't nearby, and he showed us into his kennel. There was a chest of drawers, a table and four chairs in his living room, all made from the same thick wood as his door.

We sat down and Bones took out his notebook.

"It sounds like you saw the villain," said Bones. "Could you describe them for us?"

Butch cowered in his chair and peeped at us from between his paws. "I can't," he said, in an uneven voice. "He was too horrible."

I wondered what kind of monster we were looking for. If a massive dog like this Doberman was scared, then the thief must truly be a fearsome beast.

"Just try your best," I said. "We can only catch him with your help."

"Okay," said Butch. He lowered his paws. "I was in my bedroom on Wednesday night at around eight, when I heard a scuffling from downstairs. I came down to find the terrifying thing in this very room."

Bones scribbled in his notebook.

"His fur was matted with mud and he had nasty little eyes," said Butch. "He had a thick black tail, large ears, and sharp, werewolf-like teeth. He grabbed my priceless pocket watch from that chest of drawers and escaped out of that window."

Bones turned the page and sketched some pictures of the villain based on the Doberman's description.

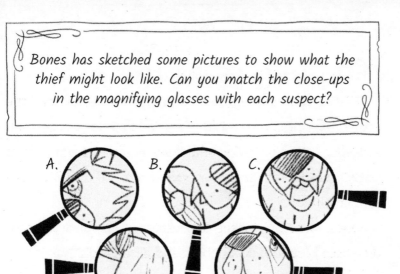

"Didn't you try and stop him?" I asked.

"I begged him to give it back," said Butch. "But you should have heard his barks. They were so ferocious."

Bones stopped drawing and looked up at the dog.

"What about the police?" he asked. "Didn't you call for them?"

"Yes," said Butch. "But the Inspector just sent round a bunch of bloodhound puppies, and all they did was have a jumping competition out of the window."

"I'm sorry you had to deal with those fools," said Bones.

"They weren't much help to Carol and Pat either," said Butch. "Or Mrs Woods, or the Taylors."

"You mean there were other victims before you?" yapped Bones. "Why didn't the Inspector tell me about all this?"

Now that Butch mentioned it, I had read quite a few stories in the paper about thefts in Kennel Heights. I thought it better not to admit this to Bones while he was angry.

"Tell me everything you know about this crime spree," said Bones, hunching over his notebook. "Every detail could be important."

"Well, Carol and Pat were first," said Butch. "They are the wombats from number 166. They were putting their kids to bed at eight o'clock last Saturday when they heard a noise from downstairs. They rushed down to discover that Carol's wedding ring had gone missing."

"But they didn't see the thief's face?" asked Bones.

"I don't think so," said Butch. "I tried to speak to Carol about it the next day, but she was really upset. The police pups had been to investigate, but they'd spent the whole time chasing the little wombats around the garden."

"Idiots," muttered Bones.

"At eight o'clock on Sunday the thief struck again," said Butch. "He stole a golden racing medal from Mrs Woods, the greyhound from number 121. She caught a brief glimpse of a vicious creature with muddy fur."

I glanced out at the sleepy street. It seemed extraordinary that such a quiet area could have suffered so many horrible crimes.

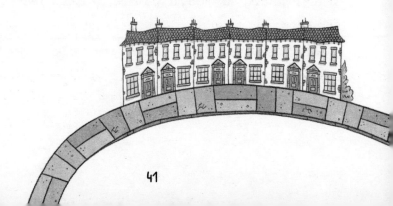

"Then on Monday at the same time, the thief stole two silver brooches belonging to Mrs Taylor, the vole from number 148," said Butch. "She got a good look at the criminal, and even drew a picture for the police pups. But they fought over who should carry it back to the station and ended up ripping it to pieces."

Bones growled and shook his head.

"We were all worried he would strike again on Tuesday," said Butch. "There was a terrible storm blowing, and the thunder might have provided good cover for his crimes. But nothing happened."

"Interesting," said Bones, jotting in his notebook. "Very interesting."

"We thought the robberies might have stopped," said Butch. "But then ... he came here ..."

Butch broke into sobs again and Bones strode over and placed a paw on his shoulder.

"Thank you," he said. "You've already been a great help. With any luck, we should be able to catch the horrible criminal soon."

"I hope so," said Butch. "I don't want anyone else to go through what I did."

Bones stayed silent as we walked back down the hill and across the bridge. I knew better than to interrupt him when he was puzzling his way through a crime, so I amused myself by watching the passing crowds.

Lunchtime was approaching, and the slug and millipede stalls were doing good business. A chipmunk on a rattling bicycle was speeding carelessly along, forcing everyone to leap aside as she approached. And a group of otters were taking turns to dive into the river below, sending up huge splashes of water.

When we were back in Barker Street, Bones opened his drawer of chewing bones and pulled out the largest one. This was always a sign that we were in the middle of a difficult case and he needed time to think.

Can you put Sherlock's chewing bones in order from smallest to largest?

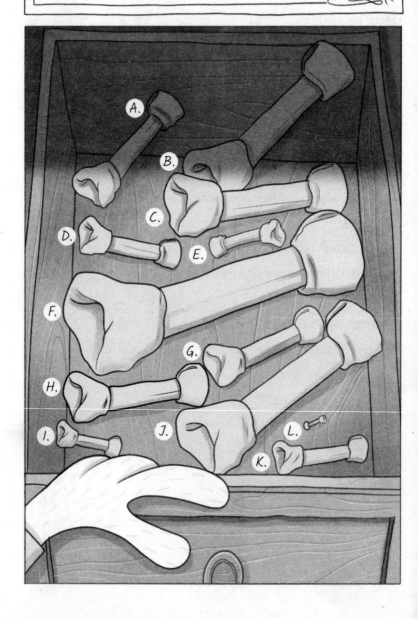

I have to admit, it made little sense to me. A mad dog had taken to stealing from the rich animals in Kennel Heights, and had got so carried away he'd eventually stolen the crown jewels.

But what did we really have to go on? The dog was big and filthy, but there would be hundreds of dogs fitting that description in the endless, winding alleys of our city. He'd stolen every night at eight o'clock, except for Tuesday, when it had been raining. That seemed to be of interest to Bones, though I couldn't make anything of it.

Just as it was getting dark outside, Bones leapt up, grabbed his violin and played a few notes. He often does this when he's had a big breakthrough on a case, so I threw my newspaper down.

"Half past seven," he said, pointing at the clock on the wall behind me. "No time to lose."

He ran into the bathroom and emerged carrying a full bucket of water.

"Where are we going?" I asked, leaping up and grabbing my things.

"Back to Kennel Heights," he said. "I believe the thief is about to strike again!"

Chapter Five

Bones flagged down a cab. We leapt inside and the toad driver steered us through the streets.

Bones told me to look after the bucket of water, and I tried to hold it steady as the vehicle clattered over the cobbled roads. A thick fog was drawing in as we approached the river, so we slowed down. I was quite glad, as it made the bucket easier to handle, but Bones was growling and fidgeting.

"Get a move on," he barked.

"Not in this weather," croaked the toad. "You might want to risk running someone over, but I don't."

As if to prove his point, a weasel in a raincoat emerged from the fog in front of us, and the toad had to slam on his brakes.

Guide the toad's cab safely through the fog to get to Kennel Heights, avoiding obstacles along the way.

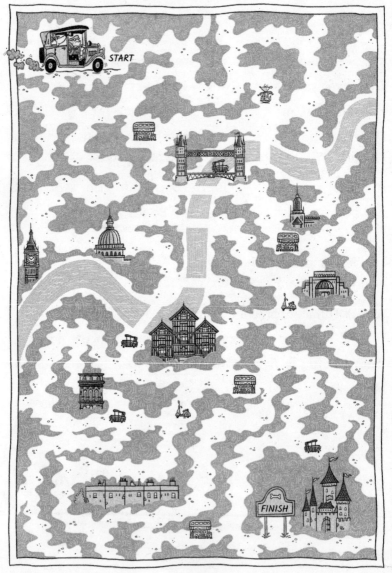

After a loud argument with the weasel, the toad got going again, and we made it to the other side of the bridge and up the winding road of Kennel Heights.

Bones asked the toad to stop, tossed him a pound coin and jumped out.

The fog was just as thick up there as it had been on the bridge, and I struggled to work out where we were. Bones strode on ahead, and I followed behind, lugging the bucket.

The street was deserted, and I could hear nothing but the echo of our pawsteps. Yet I couldn't stop myself from imagining the horrible muddy beast that Butch had described. It could be lurking anywhere in the fog, waiting to chomp on us with its werewolf teeth.

I told myself I was a tough kitty and had nothing to fear. But I still felt my tail straighten as I imagined the beast's beady eyes staring at me from every shadow.

"Here we are," said Bones.

The fog lifted a little, and I saw we were back outside Molly's kennel.

"Do you think the robber is going to strike here again?" I asked. "Shouldn't we go in and warn Molly? Her other tiaras could be at risk."

"No," said Bones. "We won't interfere just yet."

My heart raced as I thought of that poor poodle waiting in her kennel as the beast closed in. Was Bones using her as bait?

I listened for approaching pawsteps, but could hear nothing except the distant spluttering of cars in the city below.

Then I heard something much closer. A deep, snarling growl. I glanced around, terrified that the filthy criminal was crouching somewhere behind me. But we still seemed to be completely alone.

There was a creaking noise from straight ahead of us. Molly's door opened and a muddy dog emerged.

"The burglar," I hissed. "He's been in Molly's house. We must check if she's safe."

"No need for that," whispered Bones. He grabbed the bucket of water and rushed forward.

The beast spotted us and snarled. I could feel my fur standing on end. He was as horrible as Butch had said. There was a cruel, savage look in his eyes, and his long teeth looked as sharp as pins.

Bones wasn't afraid, however. He simply drew back the bucket of water and threw it over the thief.

The burglar darted up the hill, but Bones grabbed hold of his tail.

I rushed forward to help, but as I got closer, I saw something that made me stop in my tracks. Now that the water had washed the mud of the thief's face, I could see who it was.

The thief was Molly herself.

Molly whipped forward, leaving Bones holding just the long black woollen tail that had been part of her disguise. I leapt on to her, and got hold of her back legs. But she wriggled away, leaving two large boots behind.

Here are the soles of the boots that Molly was wearing. Can you work out which pair of prints they made below? Remember, the prints will be the other way around!

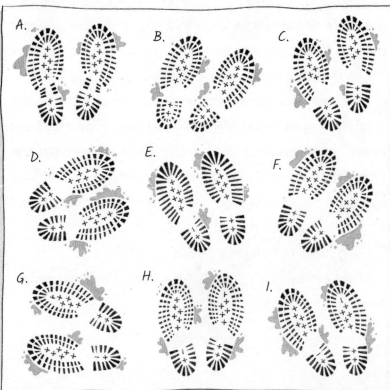

Molly sprinted up the hill. I was glad we'd taken a cab this time, as it meant I had enough energy to race after her.

Lights were going on inside the kennels, and a family of anteaters in pyjamas were peering out of their window to see what the trouble was.

I was gaining on Molly, so I took a gamble and pounced. She dodged aside, but I managed to grab her left ear. It tore away in my paw, and I found myself holding a thick strip of black wool that had been woven into a long, pointed shape.

I threw it away, and kept sprinting along the winding cobbles. I drew close again, and this time I didn't miss my chance. I jumped and sunk my claws into Molly's flanks, pinning her body to the ground.

She lashed her head around and snapped at my arm. I was expecting her strong, sharp teeth to pierce my skin, but I only felt a blunt prodding. I glanced down and saw some matchsticks that had been painted white. Of course! The teeth had been part of the disguise, too.

Molly tried to wriggle free, but I held firm.

"The game's up," I said. "It looks like your wicked performance is over."

Chapter Six

Bones emerged from the fog.

"Good pouncing, Catson," he said. He took his whistle out of his pocket and blew it.

I glanced around and saw that we had ended up back outside Butch's kennel. The door opened slightly, and his snout emerged through the gap.

"Hello?" he asked in an unsteady voice. "Is anyone there?"

"It's us," said Bones. "We need your help. Go down to the police station and fetch Inspector Bloodhound for us."

Butch stepped outside on trembling legs. He pricked up his ears and gazed from left to right.

"But what if the burglar attacks me?" he asked.

"We have your thief right here," said Bones.

Butch crept over to us and prodded Molly with his shaky front paw. She snarled at him and he flinched back.

"Wait a moment," said Butch. "Aren't you Molly Ruffington?"

"It is I," she said. "I expect you recognize me from one of my many stage roles."

"No," said Butch. "One of your parcels was accidentally delivered to me last year and I took it to your house. Remember?"

Butch drew himself up to his full height and pushed his chest out as he turned to us.

"Ah, yes, I see," he said. "The whole burglar thing was just a disguise. I wasn't that scared really."

"Anyway, there's nothing to fear now," said Bones. "Now, go fetch."

Butch darted away down the winding road.

Can you help Butch get to the police station by only stepping on cobblestones that have five sides and are next to each other? Start on the black cobblestone next to Butch.

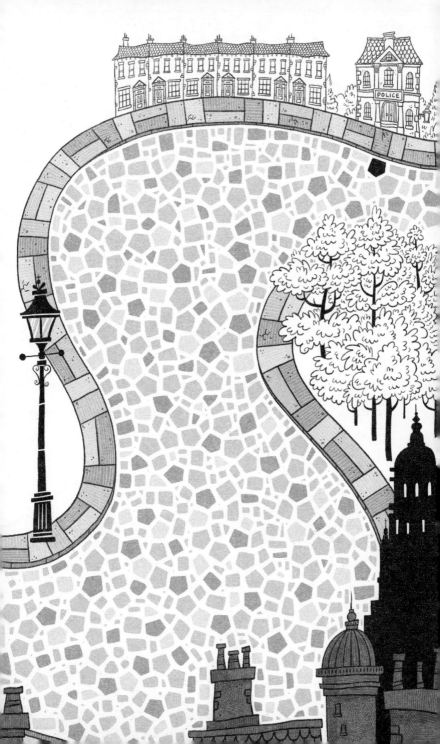

"I can convince the cleverest theatre audiences of anything," said Molly. "So how did you two fools see through my greatest role?"

"It was all rather simple," said Bones. "I was suspicious when the trail of prints ended at your door, but they didn't match your shoes, so at first I thought you were telling the truth. However, I noticed that the balls of fur at the bottom of your feet looked odd, as if they'd been pushed out of shape. It made me wonder if you'd recently been wearing some much larger boots."

Molly twisted around under my paws, but I held on to her firmly.

"Next, I noticed the posters on your wall," explained Bones. "They were all from many years ago, which made me think that your acting work might have dried up. And yet you hadn't needed to sell any of your valuable tiaras. It simply didn't add up."

"I was just resting between jobs!" yipped Molly. "The public love me!"

"The only jobs you'll be resting between now are scrubbing the prison floor and cleaning out the toilet bucket," I said.

Molly snarled.

"You also mentioned that you'd sent the local post stoat to fetch us," continued Bones. "Yet when we left your house, I noticed that the stoat was only just beginning his rounds. So you hadn't asked him to find us at all. You'd simply spotted us coming and hidden one of your tiaras, so you could make up the story about it being stolen. By presenting yourself as a victim, you hoped to distract us from the truth that you were actually the criminal."

Molly was truly a despicable liar. When she was sobbing and telling us about the theft, it hadn't crossed my mind that she could be inventing it all on the spot.

Bones pointed over to Butch's kennel.

"The final clue came when we spoke to that Doberman," said Bones. "He said there had been a dreadful storm on the only night the thief didn't strike. At first I couldn't work out what kind of a thief would be put off by rain. Then I realized. It was one who didn't want their disguise to wash off."

"Well, maybe I did borrow a few items from my neighbours," said Molly. "Though I was planning to pay them all back when my acting work picked up again. But if you think I would ever steal the Queen's crown, you're wrong! I have too much respect for Her Majesty to do that."

She sounded like she was telling the truth, but I knew better than to believe her now.

"Nonsense," I said. "We followed your trail all the way from the palace to your house!"

"I passed the palace on my way back from the Corgi Café, where I'd sold Butch's pocket watch to a Great Dane for twenty pounds," said Molly. "But I didn't go inside, and I didn't take anything."

I could hear a loud chugging engine below us. A large vehicle was climbing up Kennel Heights.

"Take no notice of her," I said. "She's lying again."

"Perhaps," said Bones. "But we have two other clues to follow. I won't make my mind up until I have all the evidence."

Inspector Bloodhound's van emerged through the fog. He was sitting at the front, next to Butch, while the police pups were in the back, sticking their heads out through the bars on the windows.

The Inspector pulled the van to a stop and the pups leapt out, chasing each other in circles. The Inspector climbed down and plodded over to Molly.

"So, this is the thief who stole from the Queen?" he asked.

"She is undoubtedly a thief," said Bones. "Whether she stole from the Queen remains to be seen. Hold her at the station and we'll come for her when we're ready."

I dragged Molly to her feet and marched her over to the van.

"You can let go now, Catson," said the Inspector. "The police pups will take it from here."

I took no notice. I knew Molly would escape if I gave the pups even the smallest bit of responsibility. I shoved her into the back myself and watched as the Inspector locked the door.

Chapter Seven

We were up early the next morning. Bones ate his usual dogfood omelette and I was about to tuck into a plate of smoked salmon when he grabbed his hat and made for the door.

"No time to waste," he said. "Straight on to the next clue. We're going to find out about that rumbling noise the shopkeeper heard."

I hurried after him, gulping down my fish as I went.

We rushed down to the end of Barker Street and headed into the park. Instead of continuing on to the palace, this time we headed north, crossed Prince Rex Road and turned into Kitten Mews.

This was a small street with a row of shops on one side and a café on the other. The souvenir shop the Inspector had told us about was the first on our right. It was called A. F. Gibson's Souvenirs and Gifts and had tall windows on either side of a red door. Mugs and plates, all of which showed the grumpy face of the Queen, were displayed in the windows.

Bones pushed the door open and a bell rung. A small mole with round glasses and a brown jacket and waistcoat waved at us from behind the counter. Further goodies bearing the face of Her Majesty lined the shelves, including spoons, thimbles and fridge magnets.

I approached the counter, while Bones examined the shop.

"Hello miss," said the mole. "How can I help you?"

"I'm investigating a robbery," I said. "According to the police pups, you've heard a suspicious rumbling noise in the last week or so?"

The mole shot out from behind his counter and leapt in front of a table covered with porcelain figurines of the Queen.

"Those police pups aren't coming back, are they?" he asked. He trembled so much that he had to shove his glasses up the bridge of his snout. "They could have destroyed hundreds of pounds' worth of stock last time. They were jumping on the tea sets, chewing the postcards and ripping the bath mats. One of them even knocked my lamp off the desk, but I managed to catch it as it fell."

He pointed to a small lamp with the Queen's grumpy face etched into the glass.

One postcard in Mr Gibson's shop costs 30p. Using this information, can you work out the prices of the following items in his shop?

- One magnet costs the same as eight postcards.
- One dog towel costs the same as two magnets.
- One mug costs the same as the price of three dog towels minus two postcards.
- One plate costs the same as the price of one mug plus three postcards.

"Don't worry," I said. "Those young idiots won't be joining us."

"Thank goodness for that," Mr Gibson said. He pottered back around the counter and slouched into his chair.

"Well, it started about a week ago," he said. "Not just a noise, but a real rumbling. It made everything shake. I had to box up some of my toilet-roll holders, because I was worried they might smash. Would you like one? I can do you a deal if you buy a bathrobe at the same time."

"Not just now," I said. "What do you think caused the rumbling? Could it have been a large van clattering by? Perhaps a group of bears running past?"

The mole shook his head.

"No," he said. "I've had problems with things like that before, but this was different. It felt like it was coming from under the ground. I wondered if it was an earthquake, but there was nothing in the papers about one."

He pointed over my shoulder to where Bones was peering at a thimble through his magnifying glass.

"Hey!" he said. "You're Sherlock Bones aren't you? Would you mind posing for a photograph? I could put you on towels, plates, toilet rolls, you name it. You could be almost as popular as my royal range. I'll even give you ten percent of the profits."

"No thank you," said Bones. "But you have been a great help. Good day."

We hurried back out into the street.

"Fifteen percent?" shouted the mole as I closed the door.

Bones examined the brickwork of the building through his magnifying glass.

"I'll keep looking for clues," he said. "You check with the other shopkeepers to see if they heard the rumbling, too."

I nodded, and continued along to the next shop, which was called Baxter's Bicycles. Inside was a large collection of bikes that filled almost every inch of the space. They ranged from giant, bear-sized bikes to tiny ones for hamsters and voles.

A young meerkat, who was sorting through a box of nuts and bolts behind the counter, looked up at me. Her fur was almost black with oil.

"Good morning," she said. "I expect you'll be looking for one of our new cat bicycles."

She got up and strolled over to a small vehicle with rope wrapped around the frame.

"This one's just in," she said. "It's got plenty of space at the back for your tail, the middle doubles up as a scratching post, and there's a net at the front for catching mice."

"It looks very impressive," I said. "But I'm actually here to ask if you've heard a rumbling noise recently."

"Oh yes," she said. "It's been going on for a while now, but it's become stronger than ever recently. It's hard to work on the bikes when they're shaking around so much."

Next, I tried the Insect Grill on the other side of the road. It was empty except for a small group of hedgehog gardeners with muddy prickles, who were eating fried caterpillar rolls.

A red squirrel in a white apron stepped forward and pulled out a chair for me.

"Can I interest you in an earwig roll?" she asked. "Or some millipede eggs? Or how about a thick piece of toast covered in slug jam?"

I felt my stomach turn at the mention of these foods, but I forced a smile.

"They sound delicious," I said. "But I'm actually here to ask if you've felt any rumbling in your café recently."

"Plenty," she said. "I thought the oven was about to explode at first, like that time I left the fly pasties in for too long."

The last shop on the street was called Toby's World of Carrots. It was clean and bright, with polished wooden floors and a high window at the side that opened on to a small alleyway. There were baskets of carrots all over the floor and shelves stacked with pots of carrot jam, carrot custard and carrot toothpaste.

Toby turned out to be a large brown rabbit with long ears. He was sitting behind the counter and wiping dirt from his paws.

Can you find the following items in Toby's shop?

Three pots of carrot jam Three tubes of carrot toothpaste

Two packets of carrot biscuits One bottle of carrot bubble bath

One bag of miniature carrots

"Twenty carrots for a pound," he said. "You won't get any cheaper in this town. I can deliver for an extra pound if you're having a carrot party."

"That does sound very reasonable," I said. "But I'm actually here to check if you've heard a rumbling noise in the last week or so?"

Toby stared up at the ceiling for a moment and then shrugged.

"I don't think so," he said.

"Are you sure?" I asked. "All the other shopkeepers around here have."

Toby tilted his head back and pulled at the ends of his whiskers.

"Nah, there was nothing," he said. "The others probably just heard some large badgers running past. It doesn't take much to get that lot complaining."

"Never mind," I said. "Thanks for your time."

I went outside again and found Bones examining the alleyway that ran alongside the carrot shop.

"Everyone heard the rumbling except for the rabbit who runs this shop," I said. "His ears are rather floppy, though. Perhaps his hearing isn't very good."

"Perhaps," said Bones. "But I have a feeling we should keep a close watch on him."

Chapter Eight

Bones checked his pocket watch and scribbled in his notebook. We'd been sitting in the Insect Grill all morning, staring at the carrot shop opposite. Every so often, Toby would close his shop, load his van with carrots and go off to deliver them for about half an hour.

"What do we notice about our rabbit friend so far?" asked Bones.

"He's selling a lot of carrots," I said. "Hardly surprising. His prices are very good."

I heard the rumbling of an engine. Toby drove back into view, parked his van outside the shop and went back in.

"Yes," said Bones. "That's certainly true. But I also can't help wondering how he can make so many deliveries without his supply ever going down. He's carried away four full van loads so far, enough to empty his shop twice over. Yet the stock we can see through the window doesn't seem to have gone down at all."

Bones was right. I could see that the baskets on his tables were still full.

It takes Toby ten minutes to deliver one basket of carrots. How long would it take Toby to deliver all the baskets outside the shop, including the basket he's holding?

"Ahem."

I turned around to see the red squirrel who ran the café staring at us with her paws on her hips.

"Far be it from me to interrupt your conversation, sir and madam," she said. "But you've been in here for three hours now and it's about time you ordered something."

Bones took his hat off and bowed his head.

"Please forgive us," he said. "We'll both have today's special, whatever that might be."

"Finally," said the squirrel. She scampered away through the double doors into the kitchen.

"Now, think carefully," said Bones. "Do you remember seeing any back doors in the shop that might have led to a storeroom?"

"No," I said. "There was nothing along the wall, no cellar door, no ladders or signs of an attic."

Toby was shifting big sacks of carrots around in the shop.

"I need to get a good look in there," said Bones. "Let's sneak in when that rabbit makes his next delivery. He locks the door, but doesn't close that side window. Do you think you could jump through it?"

I nodded. The window was high, and quite narrow. But I was confident in my pouncing skills, and pretty sure I could make it.

A damp, stale smell wafted into my nostrils. The squirrel was wandering over to us with two large pies, which seemed to be moving slightly.

"There you go," she said, placing them down. "Two specials. Let me know if you need any earwig mustard or centipede salt."

I winced, and pierced the pie with my knife. A caterpillar poked its head out and crawled back inside.

"Lovely and fresh, those pies," said the squirrel from the other side of the café. "Eat up."

I glanced over at Bones, who was tucking a napkin into the front of his shirt.

"Do as she says," he hissed. "We mustn't do anything to draw attention to ourselves."

I scooped a caterpillar, along with some crust and gravy, on to my fork and shoved it into my mouth. I could feel the disgusting creature wriggling as it went down my throat.

Bones cut a corner off his pie, and a slug emerged. He pierced it with his fork, chewed it and wrinkled his nose.

"I've had worse," he said. "I once survived on nothing but moss for a month in the Himalayas. I'd have killed for a slug then."

I sliced deeper into my pie, unleashing an army of ants, beetles and earwigs. Over at the counter, the squirrel was smiling at us with her arms folded across her apron. She'd obviously put a lot of effort into her cooking, and I felt bad that I couldn't enjoy it as much as she wanted me to.

Which of these pies does the squirrel find the most delicious? Count all the insects in each pie and then add up their points to find out. The pie with the highest total is the tastiest.

"Look," said Bones, pointing out of the window. "Toby is leaving again. This is our chance."

I glanced outside to see Toby climbing back into his van. I let the fork of wriggling horrors fall back to my plate and breathed a sigh of relief.

"That was delicious," said Bones, handing over two pounds to the squirrel. "But I'm afraid we have urgent business to attend to."

"Are you sure you don't want me to put those in a takeaway box for you?" asked the squirrel as we fled.

Out in the street, I waited for Toby's van to turn into the main road before padding around to the alley at the side of the shop. There was no one there, so I decided to risk it.

I fixed my eyes on the high, open window and crouched down. I lifted my tail in the air and wiggled my haunches from side to side. Then I launched myself up, stretching my paws high over my head.

I flew in a steep arc, passing through the narrow gap of the open window and plummeting down on to a basket of carrots. I felt a couple break under my weight, and I hoped Toby wouldn't notice when he returned.

There was a spare set of keys hanging from the back of the counter on a metal loop. I carried it over to the door and opened it.

Which of these keys will fit the lock in the shop door? Look carefully at the silhouette of the lock and work out which key will slot into it perfectly.

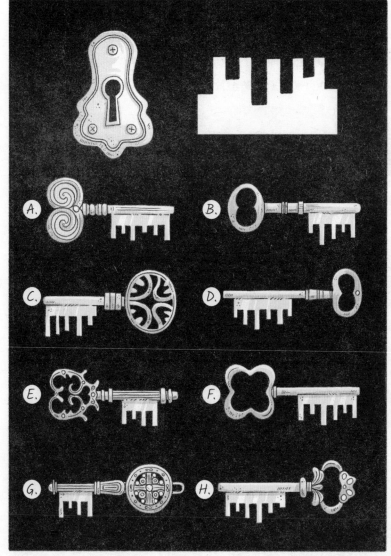

"Excellent pouncing, Catson," said Bones. "I'll examine the shop while you keep lookout."

Bones made for the back wall and tapped it with his paws.

I went out into the street and glanced around. A couple of beavers in sailor suits were making their way towards us, and I tipped my hat to them.

I was worried they might be heading for the carrot shop, but they turned into the café instead.

After a few minutes, I heard an engine spluttering on the main road, and ran around the corner to see who it was.

I gasped. Toby was on his way back. The delivery must have been quicker than all his other ones.

My fur stood on end, and for a moment I was so startled I couldn't move. Then I snapped out of it and hurried back to the shop.

Bones was on his paws and knees next to a large cupboard on the back wall.

"He's coming!" I shouted.

I was about to tell Bones to rush out, but I could hear the van drawing closer. Toby would see us if we left now.

"We need to hide!" yelled Bones.

Chapter Nine

I locked the door and returned the keys to the hook behind the counter.

"In here," whispered Bones.

He was holding the cupboard door open and beckoning me in. I managed to jump in and shut it just as Toby's key turned in the lock.

I held my breath and stood completely still in the darkness. Toby was whistling and padding over the floorboards. Next to me, Bones was fidgeting and I wanted to tell him to stop, but I was afraid to make a sound.

The whistling cut out, and I could hear Toby rifling through the drawers of the counter. He seemed to be searching for something. I was scared he'd look in the cupboard next.

Bones brushed against my legs. He'd knelt down and was scrabbling around on the floor. I was sure he'd bump against the cupboard door and give the game away. Then there was a faint clatter, and a soft thud.

I shuffled over to where I thought Bones was, but there was nobody there. I was alone in the tiny space.

I could hear Toby pacing towards the cupboard. I was about to be discovered. The rabbit was going to be angry, and I'd have no way to explain what I was doing there.

Suddenly, something tapped my ankle. I glanced down and saw what looked like a dark shadow emerging from the floor. It was Bones' paw, sticking out of a trapdoor. So that's where he'd vanished to.

I scrambled down after him, and landed on a soft mound of earth. Bones pulled the trapdoor closed just as the cupboard door above us was opening.

I was terrified that Toby had heard us. But he soon closed the door and creaked back over the floorboards.

I rubbed my eyes and looked around. We were at the start of a tunnel that curved downwards. There were no lights, but there were patches of glowing green along the sides.

"Well," said Bones. "Looks like there was more to our rabbit than met the eye. Let's see what he's got down here."

Bones set off down the tunnel, and I followed, feeling my way along with my left paw. After a few steps, the side curved steeply away. A fresh, grassy smell mingled with the soil.

"There's something here," I whispered.

I stumbled into a large space that had been hollowed out. Something struck my shoe and I bent down to feel it. A small, solid shape that was narrower at one end. A carrot.

How many carrots can you
count in the jumble below?

"Toby has hundreds of carrots in here," said Bones. "That explains his never-ending supply. He must be getting them from an illegal source if he needs to keep them hidden."

Bones stepped back out into the tunnel and continued down it. "Let's see what else he's hiding."

I felt my back stiffen at the thought of going further underground. I'd heard tales of unspeakable monstrosities lurking in the sewers and passages beneath our city. I knew they were just silly stories spread by giddy kittens, but it was hard to shake them from my mind.

"Perhaps we should go back up to the shop?" I asked. "Toby might have gone again now."

"I never run away from a mystery," said Bones. "Nor should you."

I felt my tail quiver as I trod over the lumpy ground, following the glowing green streaks on the walls. The air was getting colder as we ventured deeper.

"We're far under the city now," said Bones. I could hear him hitting the sides of the tunnel. "The soil is harder and thicker. It must have taken Toby a long time to dig through."

The tunnel opened out to my left again. Another chamber. It wasn't as full as the first, but there were still several crates and empty cloth sacks inside.

"Another store room," I said. "Interesting."

I felt my way back into the tunnel, and we kept going.

After a few moments, I thought I could hear something, so I stopped to listen. I felt like I could make out faint, shuffling pawsteps.

"Keep up," said Bones.

"Listen," I said. "Can you hear that?"

Bones came to a halt too, but the sound cut out. There was nothing but the distant rumble of cars on the street far above us.

"Never mind," I said.

We carried on, passing more long, green marks on the walls. Before long, Bones came to a sudden stop and I almost bumped into him.

"I think you were right," he whispered.

The noise was much clearer now. A heavy padding, mixed with a horrible sniffling. It was right ahead of us.

My fur prickled and my paws felt clammy. We were trapped in a narrow space, and something was coming straight at us.

"Perhaps we should go back to the shop," said Bones.

In the tunnel far ahead of us, just where it started to curve upwards again, a glowing green blob emerged. I rubbed my eyes, hoping I was imagining it.

"Are you seeing that, too?" I asked.

"Back away," whispered Bones. "It hasn't spotted us yet."

87

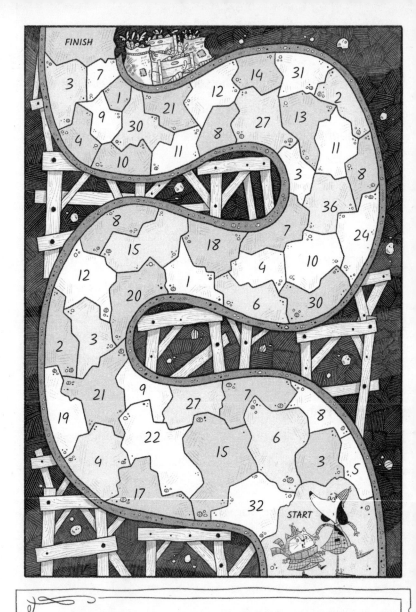

Can you help Bones and Catson get back through the tunnel? You must only step on patches of earth that contain multiples of 3 and are next to each other.

88

My instinct was to turn around and keep running until I got back to the trapdoor, but I knew Bones was right. Any sudden movements would only grab the attention of whatever monstrosity was lurking there.

I walked slowly backwards, keeping my eyes on the shape. It stayed still. We just needed to keep going back until we reached the shop, and never return to this terrible place again.

With my next step, my foot landed awkwardly on an uneven clod of earth and I toppled to the side. I tried to grab the wall, but my paws slid along it. I couldn't stop myself thudding to the ground.

I lay in silence for a moment, desperately hoping the beast hadn't heard.

It had. A screech echoed down the tunnel. The scuttling and sniffling started again, now much louder and more frantic.

"It knows we're here," cried Bones. "Run!"

Chapter Ten

I fled down the dark tunnel, terrified that I would trip over again and the monster would be upon me. A quick glance over my shoulder revealed that the green shape was gaining on us. It had a short, stubby snout and there were dark patches where its eyes and mouth should have been.

"Here," said Bones, grabbing my elbow.

He dragged me sideways into a wide space that must have been the second storage chamber.

"We can't outrun it," he whispered. "But we might be able to hide from it. This should help you hide your scent."

He handed me one of the cloth sacks. I pulled it over my head. It was lumpy and uncomfortable, probably because it still had a few carrots in, but I did my best to cover myself.

Which of the tiles at the bottom of the page do not appear in the main picture? Can you spot Bones and Catson hiding in the chamber?

A.

B.

C.

D.

E.

F.

The thuds of the creature were getting louder. Trails of fine soil were leaking from the roof of the chamber. I wondered if the whole thing would collapse, burying us and the monster alive.

The beast drew closer, and I peered out from under the sack, terrified that the shape would stop and pounce on us when it reached the entrance to the cavern.

But it didn't slow down. It just hurtled straight past the cavern in a blur of glowing green.

"What was it?" I whispered.

"I can't be sure," said Bones. "But I think that might be the Sewer Phantom."

I gasped. As a kitten, I'd been told stories of the ghostly beast who haunts the pipes under the city. It's said that you can sometimes see it down plug holes if you look hard enough. But I'd stopped believing in it as soon as I was out of cat nappies. The idea that the monster was real, and we were stuck down here with it, was too much to bear.

"We need to get out of here!" I cried. "It will eat us alive!"

"Shhh!" said Bones. "It's gone now. But any more outbursts like that, and it will come straight back."

I cursed myself for letting my fear get the better of me. Bones stepped back into the tunnel and I followed him on trembling legs.

We were heading right back to the spot where we'd first seen the beast. I couldn't stop myself wondering if it was the only one lurking down there. Maybe we'd run into a whole family of the fiends.

The green glow on the tunnel walls became much stronger, making our path easier to see. I could tell that the tunnel rose ahead of us. We were surely getting close to another exit now. We just had to continue a little further and our nightmare would be over.

A distant squeal echoed behind us, and I felt my heart hammer in my chest again.

"It's coming back!" I hissed.

"Run!" cried Bones.

We sped into the unknown dark. The patches of green in the soil whizzed past on either side. I had no idea where we were going. We could hit a dead end or we could fall into a deep pit. But we had no choice but to flee the creature.

The shrieking grew louder. It was gaining on us.

Help Bones and Catson find a route through this maze of underground tunnels, as quick as you can! Watch out for dead ends on the way.

There was a solid thud ahead of me, and I heard Bones cry, 'Ow!'

I tried to stop myself, but it was no good. Bones had fallen to the ground, and I tripped over him, crashing on to my front paws.

"Up there!" cried Bones.

He pointed to the roof of the tunnel. Five thin strips of daylight were coming through. I could make out the dark, hooked shape of a metal latch across the end.

"A trapdoor," said Bones. "Help me up!"

I knelt down, and Bones climbed on to my back. His weight shifted about painfully as he fumbled above me.

The monster's paws were pounding down the corridor. We didn't have long.

"Hurry," I hissed.

"It's stuck," whispered Bones.

Clumps of earth were falling from the roof as the shape thundered towards us. Within seconds, it would have us trapped. I could feel my pulse speeding as Bones struggled around.

"Got it!" he cried.

He pushed the door open and the tunnel was flooded with light. It felt so bright after all the time in the dark that I had to scrunch my eyes shut.

I felt the weight of Bones lift from my back.

"Here," he shouted.

I squinted up and saw him leaning through the trap door with his paw dangling down. I grabbed it and he yanked me out. We were on a patch of muddy ground next to a row of cars.

Bones slammed the trapdoor shut, and fixed the outside latch across.

The creature howled in the tunnel below us, but it couldn't get out. We were safe.

I got to my feet and wiped the soil from my coat.

We were at the back entrance of an inn, on a square stretch of gravel where bikes and cars were parked in neat rows.

"Why would Toby want to tunnel to here?" I asked.

"Could it be something to do with that?" asked Bones. He was pointing over my shoulder.

The top floors of the palace could be seen in the distance, above the houses.

"The perfect place to make off with the jewels, don't you think?" he asked.

"Let's get the Inspector," I said. "It's time we paid that rabbit another visit."

Chapter Eleven

Inspector Bloodhound parked his police van outside the souvenir shop, as we didn't want Toby to spot us and bolt away down his tunnel.

I entered Toby's shop first, pretending to browse the jams, but really sticking myself in front of the cupboard to block the escape route.

Bones entered and Toby glanced around nervously with his nose twitching.

"Can I help you, sir?" he asked, in an uneven voice. "You won't find carrots cheaper anywhere in town."

"I'm sure I won't," said Bones. "It's hardly surprising when you consider how many you've got underneath your shop."

Without saying a word, Toby leapt over the counter and hopped around Bones towards the door. But he was greeted by the Inspector, who pushed him back in. The police pups bounced in too, and ran around the shop, gnawing on the carrots and climbing the shelves.

Toby sighed. "Well, I can't really deny it, can I? But I regret nothing."

"You have no regrets about stealing the Queen's crown?" asked Bones.

Toby stared at him in confusion.

"I don't know anything about that," he said. "I use the tunnel under my shop to store carrots illegally, but so what? This new carrot tax is an outrage. Why not make cats pay more for their biscuits or dogs pay more for their chewing bones instead? Us rabbits are always getting picked on."

Bones stepped over to Toby and studied his face.

"And I suppose you know nothing about the Sewer Phantom, which we encountered under your shop just half an hour ago?" he asked.

Toby burst out laughing.

"The Sewer Phantom?" he asked. "You've been reading too many fairy tales."

Amazingly, Inspector Bloodhound started laughing too, and then those annoying pups joined in. I felt like bundling the lot of them into the tunnel and closing the trapdoor. We'd see how hilarious they'd find the beast when they were face-to-face with it.

"Enough of this nonsense," said Inspector Bloodhound, sighing and wiping the corners of his eyes. "I'll take this smuggler down to the station. In the meantime, Bones, Her Majesty has asked to see you."

"As you wish," said Bones.

The Inspector took a pair of pawcuffs from his belt and snapped them around Toby's wrists.

"And Bones?" asked Inspector Bloodhound. "Try not to mention underground ghosts."

We were greeted at the door of Kennel Palace by a large, frowning St Bernard. He was wearing a smart black suit with a waistcoat, and spotless white gloves.

"Her Majesty is not taking visitors," he said. "She is very upset."

"I believe we were called for," said Bones. "We're helping out on a rather important case."

"Ah, yes," said the dog. "Forgive me for not recognizing you. I'm Jenkins, the head butler."

He held the door for us and we stepped in. I'd passed the grand building hundreds of times, but had never been inside before. It was just as extravagant as I'd expected.

We were in a large entrance hall with a high ceiling and a plush red carpet, which didn't have any cat or dog hairs on it at all. Oil paintings of old kings and queens covered the walls, and a large chandelier hung from the ceiling.

Can you work out which item in the Royal Collection Jenkins has forgotten to dust? From 'Start', follow each direction (up, down, left or right) by that number of squares. For example, 'U2' means you go up two squares. The object you end at is the one that still needs a clean.

START

DIRECTIONS:
From 'START', move D2, R4, D3, L4, D3, R6, U2, L3, U2, L1 and D2.

I hoped the Inspector never let the police pups in, as they'd be swinging from that thing in seconds, and no doubt have it broken before long.

Jenkins led us up a spiral staircase with a bright golden bannister to a set of wide oak doors. He pulled on a thick purple rope and a low bell sounded.

There was a growl from within and Jenkins pushed the doors open.

The Queen was sitting on a golden dog basket with a purple velvet cushion and a white canopy. I'd seen her image on coins and stamps all my life, and caught glimpses of her in parades, but meeting her in the fur was quite a shock.

She was a pug with floppy jowls and a stern frown. She had dark brown eyes, and her small ears were pinned back by a silver crown. She was wearing a black dress with white lace on the collar and sleeves.

"And who might you be?" she asked in a deep, gravelly voice.

Sherlock bowed. "I am Sherlock Bones, and this is my companion, Dr Catson."

I smiled and curtseyed.

The Queen stared at us without changing her glum expression.

"You'd better find my jewels soon," she said. "I can't go out and greet my subjects without them. And this tatty silver crown simply won't do. I need one that befits my beauty."

Slobber leaked out of her drooping mouth as she spoke.

"Well, I can you assure you, we're very close to cracking the case," said Bones. "We've already captured two major suspects, and we'll return as soon as we have a definite answer."

Jenkins took a duster out of his pocket and brushed the side of the Queen's basket.

"And who are these suspects?" he asked.

"An actress named Molly and a carrot seller named Toby," said Bones. "They're in the cells of the police station right now."

Jenkins nodded.

"Well, they sound like just the kind of scoundrels we're looking for," he said. "If I were you, I'd get down there and work out which one did it."

The Queen stretched her front paws and flopped her scowling head down on to them.

"You can see how much Her Majesty is missing her jewels," said Jenkins. "Get on with it."

We bowed and left the royal bedchamber.

Jenkins followed, closing the double doors and trotting ahead of us as we circled back down the staircase. Another St Bernard who was also wearing a black suit and white gloves was halfway down, polishing the bannister.

"Would you like young Perkins here to take you to the station in his car?" asked Jenkins.

The other dog stopped his work and bowed.

"That's very kind of you," said Bones. "But we can make our own way there."

Jenkins and Perkins look very similar. Can you spot eight differences between the two butlers?

JENKINS

PERKINS

We stepped back into the street. The sunlight was so bright that I had to shield my eyes.

"Are we going straight to the station?" I asked. "The Queen seems to want us to get a move on."

"No," said Bones. He pointed to the park. "We haven't investigated the strange markings the pups found on the tree yet. And I don't hurry my work for anyone, not even Her Majesty."

Chapter Twelve

We walked across the palace lawn and over the road into the park. There was a row of deckchairs and a frozen centipede stall, with a line of oak trees beyond.

It wasn't hard to find the tree the police pups had spotted. They'd churned the grass around it into mud, but luckily the marks on its bark were unharmed. They were too far up the tree for the young fools to reach.

Bones took out his magnifying glass and studied the trunk.

"What do you think they mean, Catson?" he asked.

I examined the marks. They were an odd mix of long and short scratches. Some were shallow, while others were so deep that they cut through to the lighter wood beneath the bark.

"I don't think they mean anything," I said. "The tree has probably just been used as a scratching post by a local cat."

Bones pointed to the highest marks, then to the lowest marks.

"And yet the marks at the top are much older than the ones at the bottom," he said. "Why?"

The scratches at the top had been darkened by dirt. A small spider had even made its home in one of them.

"The cat uses this park for exercise," I said. "It stops here for a scratching break every day."

"Perhaps," said Bones. "But why would your fitness-loving cat make this strange combination of short and long scratches? And why don't the marks overlap at all?"

I took a step back. The marks were ordered in neat groups. There was a deliberate pattern to them. I felt my fur prickle as an idea struck me.

"It's a secret code," I hissed.

"Exactly," said Bones. "Now, who is using it?"

He pointed at the deeper marks.

"These were made by a tall animal with thick claws," he said. "Probably a large dog."

He moved his paw down to a set of the thinner marks.

"But these were made by a different creature altogether," he said. "At first I thought it might be a small dog, but it couldn't have reached so high. Cats, on the other hand, have thin claws and can stretch themselves surprisingly far."

It was true. My aunt Ruby used to stretch herself all the

way along the dining table to make us laugh when we were kittens.

"So," said Bones. "This tree is not covered in random markings after all, but secret messages between a cat and a large dog. The thing we must work out now is what the code means."

I gazed at the marks, hoping some sort of sense would emerge. Cracking the code before my friend would be even more satisfying than catching a bird.

I could see no clues. Bones, on the other hand, had taken his notebook out and was scribbling things down.

"The most common mark is the single, short scratch,' he said. 'The most common letter in English is 'e'. So, let's suppose that the short scratch stands for an 'e'. Most of the messages from the dog begin like this ..."

He showed me his notebook. It read, "—ee— —e —e—e".

"The symbol that begins the first and second word is the same," said Bones. "Which letter would make the most sense at the start of these words? I suggest an 'm', giving us mee— me —e—e. The phrase is clearly 'meet me here'. So now we have the 'e', the 'm', the 't', the 'h' and the 'r'."

Bones went on like this until we had a full list of which letters the marks stood for.

Bones has written down a key to the code in his notebook. Using the key, can you work out what the message says? Bones has used a / to separate the letters in the message.

Bones held out his notebook to show me the complete list of the messages.

They all followed the same strange pattern, in which the dog would write something like, "Meet me here at six, I have something," and the cat would reply, "I will be here. I will bring truffles."

"Very intriguing," I said. "I expect you're about to tell me what it all means and point out how obvious it all is."

"I'm afraid I'm not," said Bones. "This one's a mystery to me, too. But I've got an idea how to find out more."

He pressed his right index claw deep into the wood to replicate the markings of the large dog, and scratched out a message that read, "Meet me at eight. I have something new."

"It should be dark by then," he said. "The cat will think I'm the dog he's been meeting, and we should hopefully get some information."

We went back to Barker Street, where my friend picked out some chewing bones and announced he was not to be disturbed for the rest of the afternoon. I took the chance to get a good nap.

We returned to the park just before eight. The last streaks of pink and orange were leaving the sky, and the lights were going on in the palace.

Bones had brought a small lantern, and he held it up to the markings as we approached. The cat had replied to our message with, "I will be here. I will bring caviar."

"Looks like we'll be seeing them, then," said Bones. "Whoever they are."

"Caviar this time, eh?" I asked. "Very pricey. What on earth could this dog be offering that's worth so much? And why does it need to be given in secret?"

"That's what I spent this afternoon pondering," said Bones. "And I have no answer. This is why we'll need to move fast when the cat arrives. If it runs, we'll have to catch it. Hide in that patch of long grass behind the tree, so we've got both sides covered."

I nodded and walked over to the grass. Darkness was falling over the park. Its pathways were empty now, and its cafés were closed.

I crouched down and waited. Eventually, a scrawny figure stepped off the pavement and came towards us. It was carrying a tin of caviar, and I got a strange, tangy scent as it approached, that I thought was ink.

Bones lifted his hat to greet him.

"You better have something good," said the cat. "This caviar doesn't come cheap."

115

The cat has been shopping at Fluffy's Luxury Food Hall. Using the sums below, can you work out how much each type of food costs?

2 oysters + 3 cheeses = £17

1 tin of caviar + 2 cheeses = £14

4 oysters + 2 tins of caviar = £32

1 oyster = ?

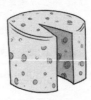

1 cheese = ?

1 tin of caviar = ?

"I'm afraid your friend couldn't make it," said Bones, stepping out of the shadows. "But I'd be very interested to know what this is all about."

The cat turned and darted back the way he'd come. I sprung through the grass and was upon the villain in three leaps. I pinned his tail to the ground with both my paws.

The cat whipped his head around and hissed at me. He was a grey tabby with three of his teeth missing and a torn left ear. He had a scar on his face, and he had small, green eyes. I felt like I'd seen him before, but I couldn't work out where.

"There's no need to struggle," said Bones. "We just want to know who you were meeting."

The cat opened the caviar and threw it at my face. I lifted a paw to stop it from going in my eyes, and he managed to wriggle free.

"Quick!" yelled Bones. "After him! He's getting away!"

Chapter Thirteen

The sticky caviar had splattered all over my whiskers and fur, so I had to stop to lick it off. As it happened, it was delicious, but I had no time to enjoy it.

Bones pointed into the gloom ahead of us.

"That way!" he cried. "Go ahead, and I'll try to keep up."

I wiped the last of the caviar from my nose, and stooped to the ground. There was a faint trail of the cat's inky smell on the grass.

I followed the scent, and it led me through a bandstand to a large pond. I heard a duck quacking in surprise and saw the dark outline of the cat on the far side.

I shot around the edge of the water, apologizing to raccoons and toads as I went.

The cat leapt into a thick patch of rose bushes. I could see only the tip of his wiry tail as he wove through.

I went in after him. The thorns scratched my side, but I felt no pain. When I'm focused on catching prey, I ignore everything else.

I emerged on to a flat lawn, and could see the cat clambering up a wall ahead. I raced after him, and scaled the wall in a single leap.

There was a row of narrow gardens below me. I could see neat lawns, small ponds, and beds of lavender and hollyhocks. The gardens all seemed empty, and I gazed at them one by one, looking for tiny signs of movement.

Can you use the following clues to help Catson work out which garden the cat is hiding in on the opposite page?

· *There is a pond in the garden.*
· *There is a watering can in the garden.*
· *The garden has more than ten flowers in it.*

121

There was something in the one to my left. A grey tail was swishing slightly behind a gnome on the patio.

I pounced. As I flew through the air, I saw the cat climb up a tree and leap on to a rooftop.

I landed on the gnome, knocking it over.

An old badger with a bushy grey moustache emerged from the door at the end of the garden.

"Gnome thief!" he cried, lifting a whistle from his waistcoat pocket.

"Sorry," I said, putting the small statue upright again. "I have no interest in your gnome. As a matter of fact, I'm in the middle of catching a dastardly criminal myself."

"Oh," said the badger, tucking his whistle back into his pocket. "In that case, carry on!"

I clambered up the tree trunk, darted to the end of a branch and propelled myself towards the roof. I caught the gutter with the tips of my claws and scrambled on to it.

The cat was to my right, leaping from the edge of the roof on to the next one along. The roof tiles rattled beneath my shoes as I chased him.

There were small gaps between the houses, and I had to time my jumps perfectly as I raced along. If I fell into one of the alleys below, I'd lose the villain forever, and probably give myself very sore paws.

The cat reached the end of the row of houses. The gap to the row across the street was too wide to jump. He'd have to stop now.

He turned and sneered at me, then launched himself off the edge. I couldn't believe he'd jumped down to the road far below. Whatever he'd been doing, he must have been desperate to keep it secret.

I raced to the end of the roof and peered over it. The cat had actually grabbed hold of a washing line, and was pulling himself along with his paws. His body was swinging back and forth as he went.

He got to the other side, leapt on to the tiles of the opposite roof and drew a claw. He grinned, cut through the line and carried on ahead.

The line flopped down to the floor, useless. For a moment, I considered trying to jump to the other roof. It would be a leap worthy of the Cat Olympics if I succeeded, but I'd seriously injure myself if I failed.

A laundry van was passing on the road beneath me. A lemur was driving it, and there was a large mound of dirty clothes piled in the open back. The laundry looked unpleasant, but at least it would be a soft landing.

I held my breath and jumped.

I landed face-down in a pile of fox underpants.

The horrible smell made me woozy and, for a moment, I forgot who I was and what I was doing.

"Ride in there if you like," said the lemur, sticking her head out of the cab. "But I won't be responsible for any damage to your health."

Through my swimming vision, I saw she was middle-aged and wearing round glasses.

"Cat," I said, trying to ignore the pong and pull my thoughts together. "Chasing bad cat."

I stuck my head over the side of the van until I could see and think clearly again. I spotted my prey racing away across the rooftops on our right.

"Follow that cat!" I yelled, pointing up. "I'm on important detective business."

"I've got my rounds to make and I'm not changing them," said the lemur. "And you won't want to be in there when I collect the socks from that young skunk at number 39. Even by skunk standards, he's a smelly one."

We were approaching a turn in the road, and if we didn't take it, the cat would get away.

"I happen to be on secret business from the Queen," I hissed.

"Ooh, I like her," said the lemur. "Really good at waving, she is. Come on, then."

She swung into the road and sped up. We were gaining on the cat, and I was worried he might spot me, so I took a deep breath and buried my head in a pile of stoat vests.

When I peeped out again, I saw the cat climbing down from the roof by swinging on metal window shutters. He reached the ground, looked around and slunk into an alley.

"Thanks," I said to the lemur. "If you see a dog in a tweed hat with a magnifying glass, please tell him where I went."

I jumped off the van and crept up to the alley. I could see it was a dead end, with steep brick walls on each side. There would be nowhere for the villain to escape this time.

I entered the alley. It was so dark I could make out nothing but the outline of a pile of wooden crates and saw a pair of green eyes on top.

"Who were you writing those messages to?" I asked. "What are you keeping so secret?"

There was no reply.

Another pair of green eyes appeared on my right, then another to my left. The sour scents of a dozen filthy cats filled my nostrils.

A car clattered past, briefly lighting up the alleyway.

Scrawny cats covered in bite marks and scars were all around me. They all looked like the one I'd been chasing, and it took me a moment to pick him out.

Can you spot the cat that Catson has been chasing? It's the cat whose left ear is torn.

"Get her," said the cat in a low, rasping voice. "There's a pound in it for all of you."

The cats hissed and stalked towards me with their ears back and their tails up. They grinned, pulling their lips back to reveal yellow teeth and cracked gums.

"Stay out of this, gentlemen," I said. "This isn't your fight."

The cats leapt on me, and I felt sharp claws digging into my skin.

Chapter Fourteen

I shook violently back and forth, managing to lose the cats that had jumped on me. I jabbed my right paw at a cat approaching from the front, and kicked my leg out to strike one coming from the back.

I launched myself into the air and flipped over twice, landing on a crate just below the cat I'd been chasing.

The cats gathered below me, hissing and snarling.

"Call them off," I hissed. "You'll only get yourself into deeper trouble."

"I won't get into any trouble if no one ever finds you," he rasped.

I heard heavy paws padding down the street and saw the familiar outline of a deerstalker hat at the end of the alleyway.

"Bones!" I yelled. "In here."

Sherlock Bones ran into the alley with his lantern held up.

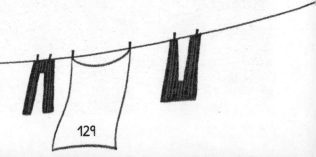

How many crates are in the alley? Make sure you count any crates hidden underneath or behind the crates you can see. None of the crates are floating in mid-air.

"There you are!" he said. "The lemur told me you were around here."

The cats disappeared like shadows banished by light.

The cat I'd been chasing tried to leap away, too, but I gripped his wrists and shoved him against one of the crates.

Bones handed me some pawcuffs, and I clicked them on.

Bones lifted his lantern to the cat's face. A patch of fur had been scratched from his nose, and several of his whiskers were missing.

"Who are you?" asked Bones. "And who have you been meeting?"

"I'm saying nothing without my lawyer," hissed the cat.

I examined the cat's scowling face. I couldn't shake the feeling that I'd seen him before. Had we caught him committing some other hideous crime in the past?

Then it all fell into place.

"You're Ashley Sloper," I said. "The royal reporter for *The Morning Terrier.* They put your picture next to your stories."

The cat looked down at the ground.

"No idea what you're talking about," he said.

"I do believe you're right," said Bones. "Well done, Catson. Perhaps you aren't wasting your time reading that newspaper after all."

The cat's face drooped.

"All right," he said. "What if I am? You've got no evidence that I've done anything wrong."

"As a matter of fact, we do," said Bones. "We know you've been leaving coded messages and offering bribes to someone outside the palace. We also know you can make a swift getaway through the park. Is that the way you went after you'd taken the Queen's crown?"

Ashley trembled, and his eyes widened.

"The crown?" he cried. "I don't know anything about that."

"Well perhaps you can tell us which objects were so valuable that you've been trading them for truffles and caviar?" asked Bones.

Ashley sighed. His rotten breath made me wince.

"Fine," he said. "But I haven't been trading objects at all. I've been trading information. Jenkins gives me exclusive stories about the royals in exchange for all that fancy food. He's developed expensive tastes eating the Queen's leftovers, but he can't afford to buy any of that stuff for himself. So he tells me what's going on inside the palace, and I thank him with posh grub."

I felt a pang of pity for the Queen as I thought about how her most trusted staff member had betrayed her.

"But I'm just doing my job," said Ashley. "The police can't arrest me for anything."

"Oh, but they can," said Bones. "You're a key suspect in the crown theft, and we're taking you to the police station right now."

We marched Ashley back to the park, then south along King's Lane.

We were soon at the police station, a wide building that had thick metal bars across the windows.

We opened the front door and stepped into the entrance hall. Inspector Bloodhound was scribbling a report at his desk, while the police pups were playing with a pot of flowers that they'd overturned.

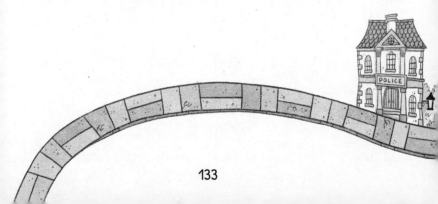

The police pups can't sit still! Can you work out which pup is missing from each picture?

 Benedict
 Bessie
Bartholomew
 Bibi
 Benjamin

A.

B.

C.

D.

The Inspector leapt up when he spotted us.

"Look after this one for us," said Bones. "We'll be back soon, but first we need to return to the palace."

The Inspector grabbed Ashley by the cuffs, and the police pups bolted over, surrounded him, and yipped.

"Are you about to reveal the identity of the thief to the Queen?" asked Bloodhound. "If so, I should be there."

"Sadly not," said Bones. "We're on our way to collect another suspect, in fact."

Inspector Bloodhound gasped.

"A villain in Her Majesty's own house," he said. "This is even more serious than I thought."

The palace was completely dark by the time we arrived. A German shepherd guard growled as we approached, but nodded and waved when he recognized us.

Bones rang the bell, and I heard paws shuffling inside the building.

Jenkins came to the door. He was wearing a purple dressing gown and a white sleeping cap.

"We allow no visitors at night," he said. "This had better be an emergency."

"I'd say it is," said Bones.

He reached forward and grabbed Jenkins' wrists, and I slapped a pair of pawcuffs on them.

"Help!" cried Jenkins. "These brutes are attacking me."

Perkins raced down the stairwell and barked at us. He was also wearing a purple gown and white hat.

"I'm afraid we're taking your master to the police station," said Bones. "You can look after his duties while he's away."

"The police station?" asked Jenkins, struggling against the cuffs. "What on earth for?"

"Does the name Ashley Sloper mean anything to you?" I asked.

Jenkins drooped his head and let out a low whine.

"Oh dear," he said. "Sloper's blabbed, has he? I suppose I'll have to find work elsewhere now. They'll be no coming back from this."

Bones yanked Jenkins outside by his cuffs. Perkins followed and watched from the doorway with wide eyes as we dragged his master away.

"You'll be working in the prison laundry if we find you guilty," I said.

"Guilty of what?" asked Jenkins.

"Of stealing the crown jewels," said Bones.

Jenkins came to a sudden stop, jerking Bones backwards.

"How dare you suggest I would do that," he cried. "Whatever else I have done, I would never take Her Majesty's most prized possessions."

Tears were streaming down the dark patches of fur under his eyes.

"We now have four suspects," said Bones. "And none of you admit to the theft. Now let's get to the station and find out who's lying."

Chapter Fifteen

Inspector Bloodhound was standing outside the police station as we approached with the final suspect.

"Not you, Jenkins," he said. "You always seemed so dependable."

"I swear I didn't steal from the Queen," said Jenkins. "The only thing I'm guilty of is making friends with a slippery newspaper reporter."

"And selling royal secrets," I added.

The Inspector growled at Jenkins, who hung his head in shame.

The police pups raced around Jenkins' legs as we walked through the entrance hall and down to the door at the far end.

The smooth white walls gave way to a long tunnel of dusty, exposed brickwork. Small lights hung along the ceiling, breaking up the gloom.

There were four cells at the end of the corridor. The first on our right was empty. Ashley was in the next. His pawcuffs were off, and he was prowling back and forth.

Molly was in the next cell. She was lying on the small, hard bunk that ran down the side of it and howling to herself.

Toby was in the one next to her. He was on his knees in the corner, desperately trying to burrow his way to freedom. So far, he's only managed to dislodge a small patch of dirt from between the stone slabs.

The Inspector took a key from his belt and unlocked the empty cell next to Ashley's.

"Here's your room," he said. "It's not exactly the palace, but it's more than you deserve."

Bones shoved Jenkins inside.

The Inspector locked the door, strode into the middle of the corridor and looked at each of the cells.

"Well, isn't this a puzzle?" he asked. "Four suspects owning up to wrongdoings, but none will admit to the big one."

"It is indeed a brain-teaser," said Bones.

"What do you suggest?" asked the Inspector. "I could send the police pups in to howl at them until they confess?"

I imagined being kept awake all night by those annoying puppies. Under that kind of torture, all four would probably confess, and we'd be no nearer the truth.

"I'll spare them that for now," said Bones. "Let me take a statement from each of them first."

We then went around each of the cells. Bones asked the suspects to tell us exactly where they had been on the night of the theft, while Inspector Bloodhound wrote everything in his notebook.

Molly's Statement

I left my kennel wearing my disguise and carrying the pocket watch I stole from that cowardly dog at number 134. I walked down Kennel Heights, crossing the river and going past the palace, then sold the watch in the Corgi Café for twenty pounds. Having shifted the stolen item, I returned home.

Although I didn't realize it at the time, I must have stepped through a puddle outside the palace, leaving the trail of prints that took you to my door. But I didn't steal the crown, and I knew nothing about it until you visited the following day.

Toby's Statement

I closed my shop and entered my tunnel through the cupboard. I walked to the end of it, where I picked up a shipment of carrots from a Swedish rabbit at the back of the inn. It was a big haul, so I dragged the crates of carrots through the tunnel in large batches. If I'd been more careful, those nosy neighbours of mine would never have heard any rumbling, and I wouldn't be caught up in all this nonsense.

I admit I avoided paying tax on the carrots, but I pass on all the savings to my customers. If it means a rabbit family with seven hungry kits can eat, is that really so bad? I've never been near the crown jewels, and nor would I consider stealing them.

Ashley's Statement

I met Jenkins at the tree and gave him a jar of truffles in exchange for the information that Prince Rex had chewed the Queen's favourite slippers, which I wrote about in the newspaper. I walked back to our offices through the park and I never caught so much as a glimpse of the missing crown.

Jenkins' Statement

I served the Queen her supper of two fried quails' eggs on dog biscuits, and instructed the maids to sweep the entrance hall. I slipped out to meet Ashley, and I passed on some information about the young prince, which he was able to use. I took my payment of truffles, returned to the palace and hid them in my room. I then checked on Her Majesty before she went to bed. All the crown jewels were still laid out on her purple cushion at that point. I only discovered they were missing when I was awoken by her howls the following morning.

When they'd all finished, Bones sat down on the chair at the end of the corridor and read through the statements in silence.

Jenkins was grasping the bars of his cell and weeping quietly. Ashley was skulking at the back of his. Molly was on her bed with her paw over her forehead. Toby was standing behind the bars with his arms behind his back.

At last, Bones spoke.

"Well, from those statements, I think it's pretty obvious who did it," said Bones. "Have a look for yourself," he said, passing the notebook to me.

I read through all the statements again, but I still had no idea who was guilty. It certainly wasn't obvious to me.

Bones turned to the Inspector. "Have you solved it yet?" he asked.

"I'm afraid not," said the Inspector.

"The thief is right there," said Bones, leaping up and pointing to the cell with the culprit in.

Chapter Sixteen

Sherlock Bones was pointing at Toby's cell. The rabbit said nothing. He just kept staring at us and frowning.

"Thank heavens!" said Jenkins, wiping tears from his eyes. "I knew you'd get to the truth."

"Told you it wasn't me," muttered Ashley. "Now, how about getting me out of here?"

"What a horrid rabbit," said Molly. "I may have borrowed a few things from my neighbours, but only a true villain would steal from the Queen."

Bones strode over to Toby's cell.

"I don't know what you mean," said the rabbit, shoving his face up to the bars. "I've said nothing that would make anyone think I was guilty."

"Oh, but you have," said Bones.

He put his paws behind his back and paced up and down.

"All along, I'd only been telling you and the other suspects that the crown was missing," he said. "I never mentioned the rest of the jewels. And that was a deliberate trap."

I nodded, even though I hadn't actually noticed this detail at all.

"In their statements, Molly and Ashley mentioned only the crown, which matches the information they'd been given," said Bones. "Jenkins knew all the jewels had been stolen, of course, so it's no wonder he referred to them."

Bones turned to face the rabbit. "But you mentioned the 'crown jewels', even though I'd only told you the crown was missing."

I thought about Toby's statement. Bones was right.

"So how did you know all the items had gone missing?" asked Bones. "Because you were the one who stole them."

I couldn't believe I'd failed to work it out. I hadn't been this embarrassed with myself since I'd jumped at my own reflection in a mirror when I was a kitten.

Toby drew away from the bars and slouched into the shadows at the back of his cell.

"Okay," said the rabbit. "So what if I took them? I'd just finished loading the carrots into my tunnel when I glanced over at the palace and noticed one of the windows was open, so I walked over to look. The guard patrolling that side had fallen asleep, and I thought I might as well climb in. I admit I was shocked to find myself in the bedroom of the Queen, and at first I was going to leave the jewels. But then I remembered how much money us rabbits had lost through the carrot tax. I thought if everyone was stealing from us, why shouldn't we steal from them?"

"You have upset the most beloved lady in the land with your crime," said the Inspector. "And I shall be locking you away for a very long time. Now tell us where the jewels are or I'll make it even longer."

I thought back to the time we'd hidden in the second storage chamber to escape the phantom. I'd pulled a sack of strange, lumpy shapes over myself. It dawned on me that I'd already discovered the location of the jewels without realizing it.

"I think I know where they are," I said. "In the second storage chamber of Toby's tunnel."

Bones looked at me in confusion.

"But if you knew where they were all along, why are you only telling us now?" asked the Inspector.

"I've only just realized," I said. "It's hard to think straight when the Sewer Phantom is on your heels."

The Inspector sighed and rolled his eyes.

"Now, now, Dr Catson," he said. "It was funny the first time, but this has to stop now. This is a very serious business."

"I'm afraid she's speaking the truth," said Bones. "There's something unspeakable down there."

The Inspector shook his head.

"You might well think you saw something down there," he said. "But your mind plays tricks in the dark, everyone knows that. This time we'll take lights, and you'll see nothing more dangerous than a few stray worms. Now, let's get going."

He stormed away down the corridor.

"It's true," whispered Toby. "There is some sort of beast down there, though it's nothing to do with me. It must have broken through from a nearby sewer. If I were you, I'd leave the tunnel well alone."

We ignored the gloating rabbit and strode after the Inspector, but I couldn't stop my paws from trembling. Whatever the Inspector thought, the fiend was real. And we were heading right back into its lair.

Can you work out which storage chamber the crown jewels are in? Use the clues to find out what to do at each object you encounter. The final destination is the correct chamber.

When you reach a group of rocks, turn north.

When you reach stalactites, turn south.

When you reach a fossil, turn east.

When you reach a worm, turn west.

N
W — E
S

START

In the entrance hall, the Inspector was handing out tiny lanterns to the police pups.

"Don't tell me they're coming along as well," I said.

"Of course," said the Inspector. "This will be a great experience for them."

I thought it was more likely to be a terrifying one that would put them off police work for life, but I knew I couldn't change his mind.

We grabbed lanterns too, and headed out into the street.

When we arrived at Toby's shop, Bones went in first, and opened the cupboard door at the back. He turned to address the others.

"Follow us down if you must," said Bones. "But I warn you that a mysterious evil is lurking somewhere in here."

He unhooked the trap door.

The police pups bombed through it with high yips, taking no notice of what Bones had said. We went in next, and the Inspector followed.

I could see the tunnel properly by the light of my lantern, and I noticed that large grooves had been scratched along the sides, no doubt by the creature.

Bones led us to the first storeroom, where the carrots

were stacked in huge piles, with their green fronds dangling down.

"His illegal shipment," I whispered. "The jewels are in a bag in another room like this, about 200 metres along. We'll need to creep up very carefully to avoid disturbing the creature."

The police pups ignored my instruction and raced down the tunnel, barking as loudly as they could.

"Call them back, Inspector!" I hissed. "They're in great danger."

"Nonsense," said the Inspector. "Let them enjoy themselves. They hardly ever get to go in any tunnels."

We crept slowly ahead, while the pups wasted their energy running back and forth. Our lanterns swung as we ventured along, casting flickering shadows over the uneven sides.

The second storage chamber appeared on our left. There were a dozen cloth sacks on the floor, but I recognized the one I'd been under straight away. It had a large lump in the middle, which I could now clearly see was the crown. The smaller lumps of the ring and necklace were on either side.

I opened it and held my lantern over it to check on the jewels. They were all completely unharmed.

Which of the following sets of gems exactly matches the jewels you can see in this picture of the Queen's crown?

A.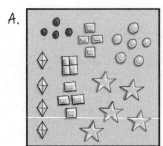

B.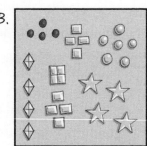

C.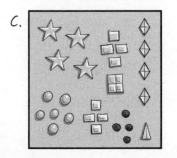

D.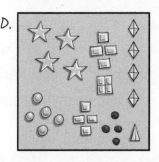

"Excellent," said the Inspector, taking the sack. His tail was wagging frantically. "It all worked out fine in the end, then."

A high squeal echoed from deep in the tunnel.

The Inspector's tail fell completely still. He gazed at me with wide eyes.

"It can't be …" he said. "Can it?"

I stepped back into the tunnel and held my lantern up. I could see something in the far distance, at the point where the tunnel curved upwards. It was the same glowing green shape we'd seen before.

The monster was back.

Chapter Seventeen

The Inspector was trembling so much his lantern was shaking, throwing jerky light around the tunnel.

"It's the Sewer Phantom," he gasped. "It's coming for us."

"I told you," I said. "Now do you wish you'd listened?"

"Never mind that now," yelped the Inspector. "We need to get out of here! Run!"

The police pups obeyed him. Unfortunately, they ran the wrong way. They were heading straight towards the beast.

"Come back!" shouted the Inspector. "It isn't safe!"

The puppies ignored him, barking as they ran. I could see the green shape picking up speed as it flew down the tunnel.

"We'll have to go after them," said Bones. "We can't abandon them to that fiend, however foolish they are."

I forced myself to go onwards, heading straight for the beast, when all my instincts told me to save myself and run.

The beast let out another shriek as it thundered towards us. I was hoping it would frighten the pups, but they kept charging forward as fearlessly as if they were chasing a squeaky toy.

"Benedict! Bessie! Bartholomew! Benjamin! Bibi!" cried the Inspector. "Stop!"

The pups took no notice.

The glowing green shape and the five tiny lanterns were hurtling towards each other.

The creature screamed. The pups yelped.

"It's attacking them!" cried Bones. "Hurry."

I propelled myself forward, even though my knees were weak and sweat was pouring down my forehead.

The pups and the monster collided. I could see their dark outlines crawling all over its glowing body. If it was attacking them, they were at least fighting back.

There was another screech from the monster. But this one sounded different. Almost as if it were laughing.

As I drew near, I could make out more of the beast by the light of our lanterns. It had a short snout, a black nose, small eyes and round ears.

Bones raced ahead and knelt down next to the creature.

"This is no phantom," he said. "That's a young bear."

Bones was right. The bear was lying on his back and giggling, while the police pups tickled his tummy. Bartholomew playfully nipped his paw, and the bear gently patted him away.

"How did you get here?" asked the Inspector.

The bear kept giggling and batting the pups away.

"He's too young to speak," said Bones. "Only a baby, really."

The glowing green colour was rubbing on to the pups. Toby must have kept the poor creature prisoner and covered it in luminous paint to make us think the sewer monster was patrolling his tunnels. The bear must have brushed some of the paint on to the walls of the tunnel too, which explained the green streaks.

Bones offered his paw to the bear.

"Come with us," he said. "We'll get you out of this place."

The bear looked over at the pups, who grinned and nodded at him. He got to his feet and took Bones' paw. They plodded back along the tunnel together.

When we got to the police station, the Inspector wiped the paint off the bear with a towel, while the pups barked happily at it.

The bear whined and rubbed its tummy. Bessie waddled over to her desk and returned with a packet of dog biscuits. The bear put one in his mouth, chewed it for a moment, smiled, then chomped down the rest.

"Poor thing must have been living on carrots for days," said the Inspector.

There was the chug of an engine, and a large golden car appeared on the street outside.

"It's the Queen!" barked the Inspector. "Get into a line, pups. And put that bone down, Benjamin."

The smallest of the pups spat out his rubber bone and joined the others in a neat row next to the Inspector. Bones and I stood at the far end.

The door was thrown open, and Perkins appeared. He was carrying a purple cushion and a wooden box.

"Her Majesty the Queen," he announced.

The Queen shuffled in. She had her silver crown on and was wearing a long black dress that swept the dusty floor behind her.

"I believe you have something of ours," she said.

"Certainly, Your Majesty," said the Inspector.

He bowed, rushed over to his desk, and took the crown, ring and necklace out of the sack. He placed them on the purple cushion, and Perkins carried them over to the Queen.

There were tears in the corners of her eyes as she pulled the ring on, and drew her necklace over her shoulders. She took off her silver crown, handed it to Perkins, and replaced it with the golden one.

She dragged her droopy mouth into a smile for a brief second.

"That's better," she said. "And we have brought something in return for your hard work and bravery."

The Queen stepped forward. Perkins hovered at her side and opened the wooden box. Inside were three large gold medals for the Inspector, Bones and I, and five small ones for the police pups. The Queen took them out and pinned them to our chests.

Using the following information, can you work out which police pup received their medal first?

· Benedict got his before Bartholomew, but just after Bibi.
· Benjamin got his after Bartholomew, but before Bessie.

Benedict

Bartholomew

Bessie

Bibi

Benjamin

"You can tell Jenkins that he is not welcome at the palace again," she said. "But we won't be pressing charges against him or that ghastly newspaper cat."

She turned to leave, and Perkins raced ahead to hold the door open.

We stayed in place and watched through the window until the car had driven away.

"I suppose we'd better let the other suspects go," said the Inspector.

We followed him through the door at the back of the hall and along the dusty corridor. All four prisoners stepped up to the front of their cells to see us.

"Hello?" asked Ashley. "Have you forgotten about me? I'm innocent, remember."

The Inspector unlocked his door and held it open for him.

"I hope you stay out of trouble and don't end up here again," said the Inspector.

"And I hope you stay out of trouble and don't end up in my newspaper," said Ashley.

He planted his paws in his pockets and slouched away.

The Inspector moved on to Jenkins' cell and unlocked it, too.

"You're free to go," he said. "Her Majesty won't be taking it any further."

"Oh, thank you," said Jenkins. He dabbed the corner of his eye with his sleeve. "I promise I'll never do anything like it again."

He straightened his nightgown and shuffled away down the corridor.

"Ahem," said Molly from her cell on the other side. "Aren't you going to unlock mine, too?"

"Yes," said the Inspector, strolling over. "And then I'm going to take you back to Kennel Heights, and we're going to visit everyone you stole from and work out how many of your tiaras you'll need to sell to pay them back."

"What?" screamed Molly. "Not my collection! They're so precious to me!"

The Inspector unlocked her cell and she stepped out, sobbing into the balls of fur around her paws.

"You're lucky that's the only punishment you're getting," he said. "You could be going to prison like our rabbit friend."

Molly's cries echoed down the corridor as the Inspector led her away.

Only Toby was left. He was gripping the bars of his cell and glaring at us.

"Better get used to those," I said, tapping the bars. "You'll be behind them for a long time."

"I see the phantom didn't get you, then," he muttered. "What a pity."

Bones stepped up to the edge of the rabbit's cell and looked directly into his eyes.

"I admit it was clever of you to disguise that poor bear as the phantom to keep everyone away from the jewels," Bones said. "So where did you get it from? Another of your smugglers?"

Toby wandered over to his bed and lay down with his paws behind his head.

"As a matter of fact, that wasn't my doing," he said. "I lined up a buyer for the jewels, but he couldn't move them out of the country until next week. He put the bear in the tunnel himself, to scare any intruders away in the meantime."

Bones leant so far forward his nose was sticking through the bars.

"Who?" he asked. "Who was this buyer?"

"He was a rat," said Toby. "He had a long black coat, a top hat and horrible sharp teeth. I think he said his name was Professor Moriratty."

Bones staggered back as if he'd been struck. He steadied himself against the wall and clutched his chest.

"Not him!" he cried.

"Know him, do you?" asked Toby.

Hearing Moriratty's name again made my fur stand on end. He was the most beastly criminal Bones and I had ever encountered. He'd disappeared a year ago, and we hoped he'd gone away for good. Now, it seemed he was back.

"Where did you meet him?" barked Bones. "How are you contacting him?"

"Calm down," chuckled Toby. "I met him at the inn, and he gave me no address. He came round to my shop with the bear later that night and told me he'd return when he was ready to take the jewels."

Bones stormed away down the corridor without another word.

"Whoops," said Toby, grinning. "I think I struck a nerve there. Why don't you go after your little friend and check he's okay?"

When we got back to Barker Street, I lit the fire, settled back into my armchair and let out a yawn. After all that running around, I was ready for a good nap.

Bones didn't sit down, however. He paced around with his paws behind his back, growling to himself.

"Cheer up," I said. "We cracked the case, after all."

"But we didn't catch Moriratty," he said. "We were so close to him, and had no idea. Now there will be a hundred more crimes.'

Bones stopped next to the window and gazed down at the dark street.

"That evil rat is lurking somewhere out there," he said. "And I dread to think what his plans are."

ANSWERS

THANKS FOR HELPING
US CRACK THE CASE.

Chapter One

Page 8-9
The answer to the word finder puzzle is 'Carrots'. The story that's caught Catson's attention is the 'Mystery at the Docks' story on page 9.

Page 12
Silhouette B.

Chapter Two

Page 21
Trail C.

Kennel E.

Chapter Three

Page 28

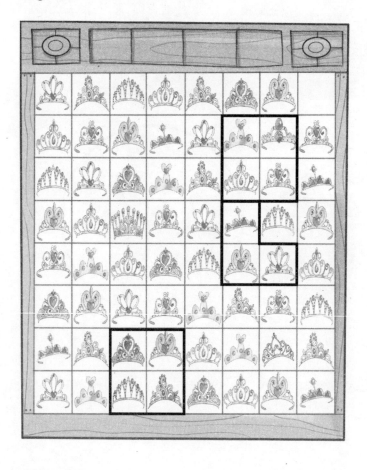

Page 33

The correct order of the panels is: A, F, D, H, C, E, B, G.

The image of Butch should look like this:

Chapter Four

Page 38–39

A. = 3.
B. = 1.
C. = 5.
D. = 2.
E. = 4.

Page 44

The order of bones from smallest to largest is:
L, I, E, K, D, G, A, H, C, B, J, F.

Chapter Five

Page 48

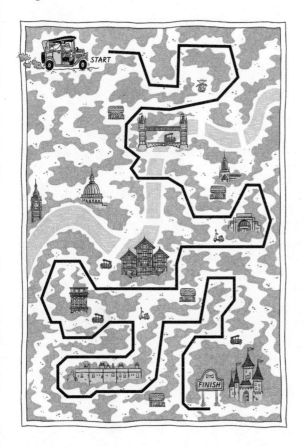

Page 52
Molly's boots match prints G.

Chapter Six

Page 56–57

Chapter Seven

Page 65

1 magnet costs £2.40 [30p x 8 = £2.40]
1 dog towel costs £4.80 [2 x £2.40 = £4.80]
1 mug costs £13.80 [3 x £4.80 = £14.40. £14.40 – 60p
  = £13.80]
1 plate costs £14.70 [£13.80 + 90p = £14.70]

Page 70

Chapter Eight

Page 74

There are 11 baskets outside the shop, including the basket Toby is holding. It will take him 110 minutes (or 1 hour and 50 minutes) to deliver all of the baskets.

Page 78

Pie A contains: 4 ants, 2 caterpillars, 1 woodlouse, 2 beetles, 1 centipede, 1 slug. It has a total of 34 points.

Pie B contains 1 ant, 1 woodlouse, 2 earwigs, 3 beetles, 1 centipede, 1 slug. It has a total of 40 points.

Pie C contains 3 woodlice, 1 earwig, 2 beetles, 2 centipedes, 1 caterpillar. It has a total of 37 points.

The pie the squirrel thinks is the most delicious is pie B.

Page 80

The key that will fit into the lock is key F.

Chapter Nine

Page 85

There are 18 carrots in the jumble.

Page 88

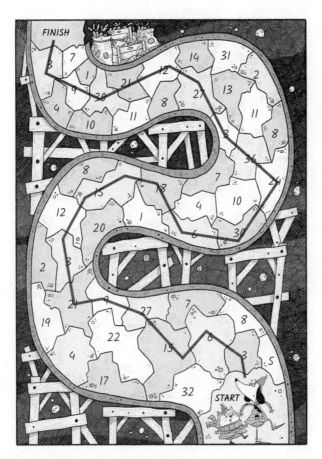

Chapter Ten

Page 92

Tiles A and E do not appear in the main picture. Bones and Catson are hiding here:

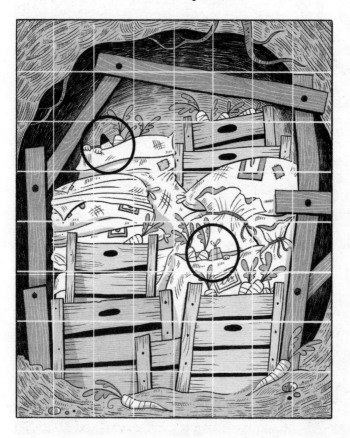

Chapter Eleven

Page 102

The item that Jenkins has forgotten to dust is the flamingo candlestick.

JENKINS

PERKINS

Chapter Twelve

Page 112–113
The coded message says:
MEET ME HERE AT SEVEN
BRING THE CAVIAR

Page 116
1 tin of caviar costs £8
1 cheese costs £3
1 oyster costs £4

Chapter Thirteen

Page 120-121

Page 126

Chapter Fourteen

Page 130

There are 44 packing crates.

Page 134

A. Bartholomew is missing

B. Bibi is missing

C. Bessie is missing

D. Benedict is missing

Chapter Sixteen

Page 150-151

Page 154
Set C matches the crown exactly.

189

Chapter Seventeen

Page 159

Pieces A and F will complete the picture.

Page 163
The order in which the police pups received their medals was:

Bibi
Benedict
Bartholomew
Benjamin
Bessie

The End!